PARTY *of* three

Also from Christopher Rice and C. Travis Rice

C. Travis Rice
SAPPHIRE SUNSET: A Sapphire Cove Novel
SAPPHIRE SPRING: A Sapphire Cove Novel
SAPPHIRE STORM: A Sapphire Cove Novel
SAPPHIRE DAWN: A Sapphire Covel Novel
PARTY OF THREE: A Sapphire Cove Suite Secrets Novella

Thrillers
A DENSITY OF SOULS
THE SNOW GARDEN
LIGHT BEFORE DAY
BLIND FALL
THE MOONLIT EARTH

Supernatural Thrillers
THE HEAVENS RISE
THE VINES
BONE MUSIC: A Burning Grill Thriller
BLOOD ECHO: A Burning Girl Thriller
BLOOD VICTORY: A Burning Girl Thriller
DECIMATE

Paranormal Romance
THE FLAME: A Desire Exchange Novella
THE SURRENDER GATE: A Desire Exchange Novel
KISS THE FLAME: A Desire Exchange Novella

Contemporary Romance
DANCE OF DESIRE
DESIRE & ICE: A MacKenzie Family Novella

With Anne Rice
RAMSES THE DAMNED: THE PASSION OF CLEOPATRA
RAMSES THE DAMNED: THE REIGN OF OSIRIS

PARTY *OF* *Three*

NEW YORK TIMES BESTSELLING AUTHOR
CHRISTOPHER RICE
WRITING AS
C. TRAVIS RICE

A SAPPHIRE COVE SUITE SECRETS NOVELLA

Party of Three
A Sapphire Cove Suite Secrets Novella

By Christopher Rice writing as C. Travis Rice

Copyright 2025 Christopher Rice
ISBN: 978-1-963135-76-3

Published by Blue Box Press, an imprint of Evil Eye Concepts, Incorporated

Cover image copyright Wander Agular Photography

Author's Note

Dear Reader,

PARTY OF THREE is a spicy, standalone story that takes place inside the world of Sapphire Cove. You don't need to have read any of the novels in the series to enjoy this novella. I've posted detailed letters about the themes explored in each Sapphire Cove story, including this one, at the dedicated website for the series, www.VisitSapphireCove.com. Please be advised, these letters might contain spoilers about the books. I hope you enjoy spending the weekend with Buckley, Mateo, and Jeff. Don't forget to hang the *Do Not Disturb* sign on your door.

Love,
C. Travis Rice

Connor and Logan After Dark

It's almost one in the morning and I've been lying awake for an hour, watching the shadows of wind-tossed branches dance on the ceiling of our bedroom.

I want nothing more than to roll over and wake my handsome husband with one stroking hand, to settle down onto the length of him, ride him fast and hard until he fills me with welcome, wet heat.

But somehow that feels like cheating.

My dream-hungry mind is a simmering cauldron of confused fantasies thanks to a conversation with an old friend earlier this evening. Satisfying my hunger without telling Logan what's driving it feels like using him. I love him too much to treat him like a toy.

Besides, we both need to be up and out of the house by seven, at our desks at Sapphire Cove by eight. With a senior management meeting scheduled for nine, we'll only have an hour, tops, to make progress on our to-do lists before the daily cascade of emails begins. Three different conferences are cycling through the resort this week, two of them on overlapping days that will stretch us to the limit. I love my job. I love being the general manager of the beautiful, sprawling oceanfront resort my family founded before I was born, the place my husband and I saved from ruin a few years ago.

But I need rest. It's not the best night to be lying awake, fantasizing about your husband making love to other men.

I tell myself I haven't done anything wrong. All I did was give an old high school classmate some steep discounts so he could throw a birthday party for his boyfriend in one of our premier event spaces. I also added a few free nights for the two of them in one of our private villas. Buckley Mitchell had sent me two thank-you emails since then, but it wasn't until earlier tonight that he called to tell me how profoundly the romantic weekend I'd gifted him had impacted his relationship in wild and unexpected ways.

The secrets he shared, the experiences he had within the walls of the resort I run, have me thinking of my husband in an entirely different way. Or silently admitting to a fantasy I've always suppressed.

I turn my head, studying Logan's profile. My eyes adjusted to the darkness two hours ago. His raw, severe beauty makes me ache. In the shadows of our bedroom, he looks like a slumbering god.

I don't know how I slept through the night before Logan Murdoch and I shared a bed. Probably by dreaming that a man of his size and strength and loyalty was pressing down against the mattress next to me. The moment you first realize you're gay isn't when the sight of another guy turns you on for the first time and it isn't during your first kiss with another boy. It's when you wake up for the first time cradled in the arms of another man after a peaceful night's sleep, filled with an entirely new feeling of completeness, of rightness.

Some days I still can't believe he's mine.

Which I guess is just a dramatic way of saying sometimes I don't feel like enough for him.

I am half his size and in the words of Logan's ornery, loudmouth father, I talk like I'm about to burp glitter.

Logan, on the other hand, is a towering mountain of a man with a voice like low thunder. Before we got together, he was a much-lusted-after top on the hookup apps many queer men use like dinner plates, a distinction that, along with his Marine Corps background, earned him the nickname Sergeant Stud. Whenever I try to imagine his wild, bed-hopping life before we got together, I feel two weather patterns slam into each other inside me, creating a fierce storm of desire. On the one hand, it turns me on to know my boyfriend was that desirable to so many people. On the other, I spent the first few months of our relationship terrified he'd throw me over at any moment for someone taller, more muscular, someone who works hard to suppress any mannerism or gesture someone else might deride as "too gay," whatever the hell that means.

It has taken me years to truly believe that I am what Logan Murdoch wants. It helps that he's done everything he can to convince me of that truth.

So why am I fucking that up by getting hot at the thought of my husband plowing random twinks in our bed?

Willing myself to sleep, I turn my back to him and screw my eyes shut.

But the hunger still courses through me.

As if he can sense it, Logan rolls over, circling one powerful arm over my bare chest, nuzzling his lips against my neck, letting out a low rumble of a groan that suggests drowsy desire. His hand travels down my bare torso, leisurely and possessively and in a way that tells me I'm his. He gently grips my thickening cock, letting out a pleased grunt at what he finds there. His hand lingers, spreading my little slick of pre-cum over the head of my cock with the pad of his thumb. I've been leaking for moments now. I fight the urge to bite the pillow. His fingers move on, caressing my balls before traveling my taint.

When he finds my hole and gently circles it, I shudder. I have always been wildly sensitive down there, and this thrills him. A live wire, he calls it. But my phone call with Buckley has left me so turned on, the charge that courses through me is stronger than usual.

"My prince is hungry," he whispers into my ear.

I want him to take me, to pin me to the bed and demolish me. But this will give the images and fantasies Buckley Mitchell sent strobing through my mind a high-definition clarity.

Instead, I roll over so suddenly, I see his eyes pop open in surprise.

"Remember Buckley Mitchell?"

Startled by this non sequitur, he bends his elbow and rests the side of his face in his palm. "Your old friend from high school? The one who'd make you go hiking and then get pissed 'cause you'd always bring several shoulder bags and a parasol?"

A CliffsNotes version of my friendship with Buckley, for sure. We were the only two gays—who admitted it anyway—at our high school, which meant we spent freshman and sophomore year treating each other like bitter rivals on a CW show. Then, right before junior year, our mutual desire to meet other guys like us made us besties, and we started speeding off to whatever SoCal gay bar we thought would buy our fake IDs. A few times, we tried hooking up, but we were so dramatically not each other's type that our make-out sessions always felt like taking too long to suck the juice from an orange slice.

"First of all," I say, "it was a regular umbrella, which is the best sunscreen there is, but yeah, that Buckley. Also, you thought he was cute when you met him at Pageant of the Masters."

Logan furrows his brow, as if he can barely remember attending the Laguna Beach arts festival at all, even though I drag him every year. "I didn't think he was cute. You asked me if I thought he was cute when we met and I said not really and you didn't believe me so you kept asking me over and over again because you get unnecessarily jealous whenever another blond bottom walks into the room."

"Only if they're under five six."

"So did you and Buckley have a fight?"

"Not really. He was calling to thank me for the party I let him have for his boyfriend in Dolphin. And everything else, I guess."

"Everything else?"

"Turns out his relationship kinda rocketed up to the next level after that weekend, and he wanted to give some credit to Sapphire Cove. And me, I guess."

"Interesting." Logan strokes my forehead, but I can tell he's trying to be patient while quietly wondering why my phone call with Buckley is worth delaying what had been cranking up to be one of the better fucks of our marriage. "Am I supposed to ask what the next level is?"

"It freaked me out a little."

"How so, babe?"

I shake my head. "I don't know. I mean, it feels self-centered. His story's not about me. Or you and me. But some of the things he said..."

Slowly, Logan pushes himself up to a seated position and then pats his thigh. I recognize the invitation. He wants me to drape my head and torso across his lap so he can run his fingers through my hair. Mostly he does this to me to relax me on nights when I can't fall asleep. Tonight certainly qualifies. Right now, I figure he's simply trying to calm me down enough so I can give voice to my tangle of thoughts.

It works.

"Storytime, it sounds like," he asks. "Start at the beginning."

The Secret in Villa 6E

1

Buckley Mitchell hurried into the tile foyer of his townhouse apartment, naked except for a pair of silky white boxer shorts.

The bell rang a second time.

Heart racing, he halted a few paces from the front door.

Turning fantasy into reality required patience, and patience had never been his strong suit. Buckley the Rocket, that was the nickname his parents had given him as soon as he could walk, inspired by his tendency to burst from the backseat of the family car and be halfway to his next adventure on little pumping legs before they could unbuckle their seat belts.

A deep breath later, he opened the front door halfway, revealing one of the most gorgeous men he'd ever seen. Even better, the guy's big brown eyes searched Buckley's nearly nude body with instant and obvious hunger. Six feet tall, with smooth brown skin and medium-length wavy black hair, his visitor's muscular torso bulged beneath a snug green polo shirt that bore the emblem of some messenger service on the lapel.

"You Buckley Mitchell?"

"Yes, sir."

He raised a manila envelope and clipboard in one hand. "Got something here for you. Gonna need a signature."

"Sure. I'm not really dressed though…"

"I can wait."

"No, come in a sec. I'm more worried about the neighbors than you, handsome."

Wearing a conspiratorial grin, the man handed over the props and stepped inside, shutting the front door gently behind him. Buckley set the envelope and clipboard on the console table, then searched fruitlessly for a pen he knew wasn't there, sticking his ass out behind him in subtle invitation.

"Here you go." Mouth at his ear, the guy raised a ballpoint pen in front of Buckley's nose. There was barely an inch of space between his chest and Buckley's bare back. "You live alone?"

"My boyfriend's at work," he lied, filling in the signature blank with a quick scrawl.

"That's reckless. If you were mine, I'd keep you under lock and key. Especially if you always come to the door like this. All naked and…" He ran a finger up the small of Buckley's back, a brief, teasing tickle that ended as soon as it began. "Irresistible."

"I'm not naked."

"You could be. Real quick."

He snapped the waistband of Buckley's boxers against his hip, then kissed the back of his neck, sending warm rivers of pleasure down his spine that melted his thighs. In a tone that was suddenly all business again, despite the fact that he'd just put his lips on a guy who was supposed to be off limits, he added, "Sender wants you to open that in my presence. Gotta confirm receipt."

Buckley tore at the envelope and removed a single sheet of paper. The message on it was simple.

I WOULD LIKE YOU TO FUCK ME HARD AND DEEP ON THE LIVING ROOM FLOOR.

It was followed by empty check boxes for *yes* and *no*.

Feigning surprise, Buckley spun to face his would-be seducer. The tips of their noses were almost touching. The man's breath brushed Buckley's lips.

The hungry stud raised one eyebrow, slowly running a finger up the center of Buckley's bare torso, circling one nipple before gently pinching it between thumb and forefinger and giving it a delicious little tug.

While he made a show of chewing his bottom lip, as if he was debating the proposition, as if good sense and fidelity were fighting a losing battle against primal lust, the swelling head of Buckley's cock appeared through the folds in the front of his boxers. The sight made his delivery man growl under his breath.

The truth was, Buckley knew exactly what he was going to do with this man.

Because his boyfriend wasn't at work.

He was right here.

Mateo Cano, the love of Buckley's life, hadn't worked as a delivery guy in years, but it was during that time, right after high school and before he'd joined the Marines, that he'd developed the fantasy Buckley was helping him realize today—a furtive fuck with a flirty, off-limits customer. Technically, Sundays were their official role-play day, and today was Thursday afternoon. But Mateo's birthday was in twenty-four hours, so Buckley was more than willing to make an exception.

When it came to making fantasies come true for the man he loved, he was always willing to make an exception. Making one exception usually left him hungry to make a dozen more.

Outside of their role-play, his boyfriend was a perfect gentleman, the kind of man who opened doors for him, placed a hand gently on the small of his back, and asked permission before stepping around him in the kitchen. They'd been together over a year, and he'd presented him with gifts for each of their three anniversaries—the anniversary of their first coffee date, the anniversary of their first kiss, and the anniversary of the first night Buckley took every inch of him while gazing up into his eyes.

Early in their relationship he'd struggled to confess to fantasies like this one. Mateo had been far less experienced then, a few hookups with guys he'd met online and never seen again. Thanks to a deeply religious family, and some homophobic commanding officers during his early days in the Marines, he'd struggled with his sexuality for years. But the more Buckley had given him the space to share his wildest side, the closer they'd become, and now, when they were in a scene, he was a filthy pig who took whatever he wanted, and Buckley delighted in being taken by him in a dozen different ways.

His favorite performances so far included a high school soccer bro, a mouthy lance corporal under Mateo's command, a pesky door-knocking Mormon missionary, and a handsy clerk at a menswear store they'd put together in their closet upstairs, complete with some potted plants and chill ambient music in the background.

Mateo stroked the rest of Buckley's cock out into the foyer's air-conditioned chill. "Think I didn't see the way you looked at me just now, you hungry little slut?" His other hand cupped Buckley's chin, and Buckley's spine went soft. "You think I don't see what a bad boy you are? All lonely and horny and home by yourself." A firm kiss, then he pushed Buckley's boxers down past his hips, leaving him stark naked in the daylight streaming through the narrow window next to the front door.

Just as they'd rehearsed, Buckley pulled away. "Alright, mister. How's this? I suck your cock for, like, a minute or two, then you hightail it out of here before my boyfriend gets home."

"Sure thing, pretty boy. Get to work." He placed one hand firmly on the crown of Buckley's head and pushed him to his knees.

Aflame with submissive desire, he tore at his boyfriend's belt buckle, then the buttons of his khaki pants.

When Mateo's cock sprung free, his wonder was genuine, even though he was only pretending to see it for the first time. Thick and veiny and proud, with smooth, heavy balls awaiting his fingers and tongue. He watched his boyfriend's every reaction as he swallowed him to the root. Watched his eyes grow hooded, his jaw tense, his breaths pulsing through parted lips.

Every now and then the pleasure made the man smile, and shimmers of Buckley's boyfriend shone through the role he was playing. The guy who brought him flowers on their second date—irises, because they represented a bright future, and because he'd listened well enough on their first date to remember purple was Buckley's favorite color. The one who loved to cook for him, who'd pull him close with one arm around his waist so he could spoon-feed him little tastes of whatever he was brewing. Transforming that sweet, sensitive man into the stuff of his most secret fantasies allowed Buckley to consume him in his purest and most delicious form.

"You know that ass is mine, right?" Mateo snarled.

Buckley stopped sucking but he didn't stop stroking. "What if we get caught?"

Mateo shrugged, but his gaze was lust filled. "I'll fuck him too, if that's what it takes to have you."

Not in the script but oh so very hot, Buckley thought, then hopped to his feet and grabbed his hand. A few seconds later, they stumbled into the laundry room like it was a storm shelter and there was a tornado screaming outside. Mateo slammed the door, then lifted him up on top of the washing machine as their mouths met in desperate, open-mouthed passion. "We have to be quiet," Buckley gasped even though they most certainly didn't and he had no plans to do so.

"How 'bout I cover your mouth when I fuck the cum out of you?"

It was a question that needed no answer. He spread Buckley's thighs, then his mouth found his hole, sending waves of heat through his body. Within seconds he was on the edge of bliss thanks to the mad, wet flickers of his boyfriend's tongue and the gentle, teasing circling of his fingers. Soon a deeper temptation claimed him. He found himself reaching for the little bottle of lube he'd stashed next to the Tide Pods on the shelf above their heads. He shoved it toward his boyfriend.

"Someone's been a slutty boy in the laundry room." Grinning wickedly, Mateo poured a thin stream from the bottle along his cock and stroked it. There was something eager and wild-eyed in the way he'd said *slutty*. Like it was a compliment on par with *beautiful*. Who was more excited by the prospect of Buckley fucking multiple strange men in their laundry room? Mateo, the fantasy delivery guy, or Mateo, the boyfriend he shared a life with? The latter thrilled him in ways that made his heart race even faster, as if there was no limit to the things they could share with each other.

His kink was being Mateo's kink.

He'd never cheat on Mateo in a million years—unless Mateo wanted him to.

"Let me show you just how slutty," he said, then spread his thighs farther in the way he knew made Mateo wild with hunger.

Once he was inside, Mateo rocked gently, slowly scratching Buckley's deepest itch. He hadn't been a virgin when they'd first met, but in the year they'd been together he'd opened a hungry place inside of Buckley that only he could reach. A good man who'd been forced to be a good boy for too long, with Buckley he could be as bad as he wanted to be.

"*Papi*, I'm going to—" Realizing he'd slipped out of character,

Mateo stopped himself. But Buckley lived for the earnest, intense tone that came into his boyfriend's voice whenever he was about to come. Like it was always a miraculous surprise to him that he'd reached the apex of bliss, a surprise that might blow them both apart if he didn't give Buckley proper warning.

"Do it."

"I'm not wearing a—"

"Breed me, delivery boy. Breed me with that big cock before my boyfriend comes home."

Utter porn debauchery, and the final twist Mateo needed. The core of this fantasy he'd been brave enough to share. Buckley understood.

Deep down, he thought, *we all want to be desired by someone willing to break the rules for us.*

He bellowed, filling Buckley with heat, body jerking as the spasms ripped through him. He barely gave himself any time to recover before he was back to thrusting and stroking Buckley's cock to completion. Then, fantasy fulfilled, characters broken, he sank down onto Buckley and took him in his arms.

The same words that always left Buckley's lips in this moment came whispering from him like a prayer. "I belong to you."

"Well, I *love* you."

"Same thing," Buckley whispered into his ear.

2

After their first date, Mateo had a crazy dream about Buckley that inspired the first couples costume they wore to a Halloween party together. It was a *Game of Thrones* kind of thing, which was weird because he'd petered out on the show after the third season.

In the dream, he was riding a horse through deep, dark woods, when suddenly there was a burst of light in the branches above. Buckley came floating down toward him, a cross between Cupid and some magical wood nymph, smiling and shimmering and shedding flecks of silver and blue that happened to be the same color as the polo shirt he'd worn to their first coffee date that afternoon. He raised some kind of wand and suddenly a burst of light enveloped Mateo. The horse was gone. The woods were gone. And he woke up painfully hard against the mattress and convinced that the guy with whom he'd only spent two blissful hours at a Laguna Beach Starbucks the day before was going to change his life for the better.

And he was right.

"Maybe shirtless was too much," Buckley said at the kitchen table. He was nibbling on a tray of cantaloupe Mateo had cut for him. This was their ritual—they'd fuck like animals and then he'd make his luscious power bottom boyfriend some food. "Like, maybe next time I'll come to the door in a tank top and you can peel it off me really slowly. What do you think? A little more resistance might amp the whole thing up. I'm thinking maybe it went too fast this time. Delayed gratification is better gratification, right? What do you think?"

Mateo smiled. Typically, Buckley would ask him what he thought of something about three times before finally letting him answer. Twice meant he was still worn out by passion.

He set a glass of juice he'd blended for him on the table, then bent down and kissed his boyfriend on the forehead. "It was perfect, *papi*. You don't need to change a thing."

"Even the best sex could use a little fine-tuning."

"Not sure that's possible if it's the best." He kissed him again, this time on the lips. "And trust me, it's the best."

Mateo was telling the truth, but he also wanted Buckley to get off his own back. No man had ever done what his first real boyfriend had done for him, created a safe space to not just share, but act out his deepest fantasies. But he was pushing himself too hard, never giving himself credit for a job well-done.

They came from different backgrounds, to say the least.

In the beginning, it had seemed to Mateo like his boyfriend's childhood had been the better one. His parents had worked themselves to the bone to support their kids while preaching fire and brimstone to them morning, noon, and night, while Buckley's lived off the sale of their start-up, got stoned at lunch, and sent him to schools where the teachers put flowers in the students' hair every morning.

But parents who set you free to be yourself at an early age sometimes forgot to give you the attention you needed, and he figured that's why Buckley sometimes talked and moved at a mile a minute, afraid of being forgotten or ignored.

He'd spent a fair amount of time around Buckley's parents this past year. They were nice enough people, supportive of Buckley's sexuality. But they only paid real attention to him when he was being funny or putting together some special project for their house. The minute Buckley started talking about something serious, something that might qualify as a personal problem, Mitch and Dana got distant. And kinda bored. There was no other word for it. The thought they might have treated Buckley this way when he was a little boy—like he was a friend who was supposed to entertain them and not their child—made Mateo's heart heavy.

As a result, grown-up Buckley was so busy trying to make everyone else happy, Mateo sometimes was left wondering if Buckley was truly happy.

"I'll tell you what I'm more worried about," he said. "Our little role-play days are feeling kinda one way. When are we doing one of *your* fantasies, babe?"

"*You're* my fantasy," Buckley said with a sweet smile.

Mateo pinched one of his baby cheeks, which was what he always did when he knew Buckley was being evasive by putting others' needs ahead of his own.

"Besides, it's your birthday. This weekend's all about you. Remember, your sister's picking you up at seven tomorrow and driving you to the hotel because I have to get there early to set up."

"Don't worry. I saved all five instructional emails." He winked. Really it had been three, but who was counting? Each one had made him smile. "Anything else I should prepare for? A water gun salute maybe?"

"I'd prefer the details of your shindig be kept under wraps until the final hour."

"Gotcha."

He turned to the cutting board he'd laid out earlier. On weekends and in between study sessions, he always prepped food for them both. Buckley's shifts as an EMT had him crawling home at all hours, ready to scarf down leftover doughnuts for dinner if it was the first thing within reach. He also hated vegetables, so Mateo was always looking for ways to sneak green things into dishes he already loved. This week's recipe was a healthy version of a taco—the meat was ground lamb, and he was blending it with zucchini he'd diced so small he'd barely know it was there. "Sapphire Cove," he said as he started chopping again. "Lotta drama at that place. Hope it doesn't fall into the sea before tomorrow night."

"Alright, now. It's had its moments, but it's doing great."

And the general manager was an old high school friend of Buckley's, so he'd probably been able to finagle a great discount on something really classy.

Lose the snark. This is going to be the best birthday you've ever had.

But there was a dark edge to his gratitude. He knew why the love of his life was really knocking himself out for his birthday this year. To make up for the two people who wouldn't be there—the parents who'd told Mateo his relationship with Buckley was *against God.*

"I'm so psyched, babe. Seriously. Nobody's ever thrown a party like this for me before."

Had he washed the second zucchini? He couldn't remember, so he ran it under the faucet. Something next to the phone caught his eye. An orange envelope. It looked familiar. It should, he realized, as he picked it up. The handwriting on it was his. The bright yellow sticker was covering up the Oceanside street address right underneath the name Jeff Braxton.

Return to sender. Unable to forward.

Rejection stung his face like a hot, quick slap on both cheeks at the same time. The Marine who'd saved his life, the Marine he'd worked for and worshiped in more ways than one, had thrown up another wall between them.

So Jeff had moved without telling him? Last he'd heard he was still stationed at Camp Pendleton, but he'd stopped returning Mateo's messages about six months ago, and he'd never been a big social media guy, so who knew?

His head spun with possible explanations, all of them dark.

Jeff thought he was a wuss for getting out of the Marines after his accident.

Jeff couldn't be bothered now that he'd been promoted to master sergeant.

Jeff regretted those few nights they'd spent in each other's arms and the awkward conversations after when they promised not to let it wreck their friendship.

The list of possible explanations could turn into a panic spiral in his head if he didn't slam on the brakes.

But he was allowed to have hurt feelings now and then. Buckley had taught him that. He'd been reaching out to Jeff for over a year, and each time he'd scraped his knuckles on a brick wall. And yeah, that hurt. No point in pretending otherwise.

The envelope contained a personal, handwritten invitation to his birthday party at Sapphire Cove. He'd placed it inside a greeting card with a beach scene that reminded him of the stretch of cliffs and sand down in San Onofre where they used to surf, a last-ditch effort to re-establish contact with a man who'd been more important to him than his own father.

And here it was, returned without a forwarding address.

Shit, Buckley thought as he rose to his feet.

He'd been ninety percent sure he'd hidden the damn thing, but apparently not.

"Guess Jeff's not coming." Mateo dropped the envelope back on the counter. Head bowed, he returned to the cutting board. It always twisted something painful in Buckley's chest to see Mateo hide his pain under a task, the way he was doing now—chopping zucchini too hard and too fast, head bowed, nostrils flaring.

On most occasions, a wondrous light came into his eyes whenever he talked about the crew chief who'd rescued him from a sinking Osprey during a training exercise gone to hell. Jeff Braxton hadn't just been Mateo's split-second savior, but his mentor as well. An older man in his life who'd actually accepted him before he'd been ready to fully come out. He'd even hung a framed picture of the two men on their living room wall, a picture that made Buckley's heart race and his skin prickle whenever he looked at it too long.

Dressed in their desert cammies, they looked like they were posing for a Marine Corps recruiting poster. With close-shorn salt-and-pepper hair and a proud jaw, the older man looked tall and imposing, his stare turned laser-like thanks to big crystal-blue eyes, arm looped protectively—maybe even possessively—around Mateo's broad shoulders. He looked so solid, so immovable, Buckley had trouble imagining what he must have looked like when he'd used all of his brute strength to drag an unconscious Mateo to the ocean's surface as the massive death trap that had almost drowned them both plunged to the dark ocean depths below.

And he'd always told himself the fantasies he nurtured about the guy were harmless, porny fun, a natural outgrowth of the fact that Jeff Braxton had saved Mateo's life.

Besides, Buckley, like so many gay men he knew, had a low, throbbing appetite for handsome, unattainable straight men, an appetite he knew better than to feed thanks to some gnarly early experiences with high school classmates that had left everyone involved more creeped out than satisfied.

Some queer men got off on hooking up with straight guys, but Buckley had always felt he could tell a guy was straight the minute he touched them. The deadness of their response could be bone chilling, a reminder they'd probably closed their eyes so they could imagine he was a girl. Buckley had no interest in closing his eyes and imagining a straight guy was queer, so the pairing never worked out.

Weird thing was, most of Buckley's fantasies didn't involve Jeff touching him, or vice versa. They involved Mateo and the man who'd been his Marine Corps mentor in a sweaty, passionate tangle, Jeff capping off his watery rescue of the younger man by giving Mateo a Hollywood-sized kiss, Mateo looking both innocent and worshipful in his arms.

But what did it matter? They were daydreams, that's all. Occasional horny flights from reality that whisked him up off the sofa when his eyes snagged on the photo during a boring moment in a TV show.

When Mateo caught Buckley staring across their apartment at the photo now, Buckley awkwardly sputtered, "So what kind of girls is he into?"

Buckley had plenty of female friends of all ages. Maybe setting one of them up with Jeff would be a good way to bring the guy back into Mateo's life.

At first, Buckley thought his boyfriend's tense expression was the result of having sensed the strange, heart-racy feeling Buckley got whenever he looked at Jeff's photo. But when he went back to chopping zucchini, Mateo had the furrowed brow and tense lips that Buckley had come to recognize as signs his boyfriend was holding back a difficult truth.

"It's probably better he doesn't come," Mateo finally said. "Our history's kinda…complicated, I guess."

Buckley's hands prickled. A question about Jeff Braxton's taste in women had resulted in the word *complicated*, and now his boyfriend looked ashamed. "Wait… You guys…"

Mateo stopped chopping, giving Buckley a wide-eyed, puppy dog look that twisted something in Buckley's chest.

"You want me to take the picture down?" he asked softly.

"I don't understand."

But he did understand. Jeff and Mateo had been more than friends. What he *didn't* understand was that in a moment when his rational brain told him he should be experiencing sharp pangs of jealousy, flames of arousal were heating up his spine and thighs instead.

"It was once or twice and it was…messy. I mean, we were never boyfriends really. But yeah, Jeff's not into women, *papi*. Like at all."

Once he'd closed the distance between them, Mateo curved his arms around Buckley's back, pulling his head into his chest. "Seriously, though, I can take the picture down if it weirds you out now. I just, it never felt like I was putting a photo of an ex up on the wall or anything because…"

"No, don't."

He'd answered too quickly—maybe because he was thinking of that time months ago when Mateo had been in a late class and Buckley had settled down onto the sofa with one of their favorite dildos and worked it into himself, his eyes landing on the photo in question while he imagined what it would be like to take both men inside of him at the same time. He'd come so hard and loud he'd been afraid the neighbors might knock angrily on the wall. And even though he'd still been a little raw from his self-love session, when Mateo had come home later that night, he'd been on him like a second set of clothes as soon as he walked through the front door, riding him hard and fast on the same sofa where he'd just done himself in.

Now, he returned his boyfriend's embrace, trying to let him know he was okay, that *they* were okay. But he didn't want to say anything to betray the strange torrent of desire unleashed in him by the news that Jeff Braxton, handsome phantom from Mateo's Marine Corps days, was as gay as they were.

And that included keeping quiet about the surprise he'd tried to put together for Mateo's party.

When the envelope had come back with a bright yellow label attached, he'd known how bad it would hurt the man he loved, and after what Mateo's parents had done a few months before, Buckley wasn't about to let someone else darken his boyfriend's birthday.

Some internet sleuthing had turned up a new address for Jeff a little ways north of San Diego along with evidence he'd been reassigned from Pendleton to Miramar, which was probably why his Oceanside address had bounced. Thinking the whole thing might have the makings of an excellent birthday gift, he'd driven an hour and a half south to Jeff's apartment in La Mesa. When no one had answered the bell at his townhouse, he'd stood for a while in the sun-drenched courtyard before slipping a handwritten note through the mail slot, a note letting him know how much Mateo missed him, how much he wanted to be back in touch, and—most importantly—inviting him to attend the party at Sapphire Cove in a week. He'd added his own cell phone number at the end and requested an RSVP.

That part was fine, he guessed. But he'd also added some embellishments along the way.

For one, he told Jeff the party started at six thirty, not seven, mainly so he could give the guy a piece of his mind before Mateo got there—let him know point-blank how much Mateo was hurt by his radio silence. A forgivable fib, he figured. Namely because his intentions were pure, and Jeff deserved a talking-to in that regard.

The second lie was a whopper, however.

He'd told Jeff the birthday party was also a good-bye party, that he'd gotten a job in Japan and they'd be moving there in a week, and this would be the last time Jeff could see the man whose life he'd saved before Buckley whisked him off to the other side of the planet.

Maybe not his best moment.

But it had been over a week ago now, and so far Jeff had made no effort to call, so he figured the repercussions would be slim to none.

Would he have jumped through several secret hoops to get the guy to the party if he'd known he and Mateo had a sexual history?

"So what happened?" Buckley finally asked. "I mean you said it was once or twice and it was messy but…"

"We weren't a match in that area."

Buckley lifted his head from Mateo's chest and gave him a smile meant to defuse the tension. "So he wanted your sweet ass and you told him it was off limits?"

Mateo's huff of laughter carried a hint of relief. "Basically, yeah."

"So what *did* you guys do? If not, you know, the full nasty."

Mateo's eyes met his, smile fading. "You sure you want to hear about this?"

"Very."

The word, and Buckley's jarringly confident tone, lit up Mateo's eyes. He looked suddenly alert but also intrigued. Buckley could hear it himself; he hadn't sounded like a boyfriend trying to clear the air after an uncomfortable disclosure. He'd sounded hungry.

There was something else Mateo seemed to notice, and the next thing he knew Buckley felt his boyfriend's hand caressing him where he was once more spilling out of the part in the front of his boxers.

"Papi…" he whispered, seemingly dumbfounded that an uncomfortable disclosure had somehow left Buckley rock hard and

throbbing in his hand.

Brow furrowed, Mateo studied him. "How's *that* going to make you less jealous?"

"Jealous was your word, baby. Not mine." It slipped out before he could stop it.

Something seemed to catch fire behind Mateo's gaze. The hungry look of a dog scenting a bone. Or maybe the relief of a man realizing he was being spared a fight with his boyfriend by a sudden, shocking display of that boyfriend's previously hidden fantasy.

Mateo's eyes glazed over. He reached up and smoothed Buckley's blond curly bangs, still damp from the shower, off his forehead. "Looks like we're finally doing one of your fantasies," he whispered, but there was seriousness in his tone. The role-play they'd done so far had involved archetypes and stock porn scenarios. Not someone real. Not someone whose last name they knew, anyway. Someone one of them shared history with. Complicated history.

"Details, please." Buckley was determined not to be swayed from his goal by the fact that Mateo was gently sliding his boxers down over his ass and caressing his ample cheeks. He always felt a little flicker of insecurity when Mateo undressed him. For most of his life, he'd been a husky boy. But apparently Mateo loved it. *Thick and juicy and soft in all the right places*, he'd often say in a hungry whisper as he revealed every inch of Buckley's skin, as if it were a naughty, hypnotic lullaby that made his mouth water.

"Well," Mateo whispered, stroking Buckley's cock in the space between them. "We hooked up twice. The second time, it was just us, and it didn't really pan out." But Mateo's eyes were downcast when he said the words *pan out*, suggesting a night more complicated and painful than his word choice implied. "But the first time was…"

"What?"

"Better. A lot better."

"Why?"

Mateo brought his lips to Buckley's ear. "Because we shared a bottom," he said.

Buckley shuddered, heard Mateo let out a grunt at the feel of slick pre-cum in his hand.

"You want me to keep going?" he asked.

"Yes. Tell me everything."

Mateo was also ragingly hard. Buckley started stroking him

inside the tent he'd made of his pajama pants.

"We went out clubbing in San Diego one night, and there was a little go-go boy who caught our eye. Jeff's got hardcore daddy energy. I mean, he can make a twink drop their undies in ten seconds flat with one look. So the guy's dancing over us for the rest of the night and we only tipped him once, but he's still hanging out. When his shift ended, Jeff asked him if he wanted to come with us, and he said yes, so we took him back to our motel in Pacific Beach."

Mateo's voice was soft, gentle and sweet, like he was telling Buckley a naughty bedroom story.

Buckley pushed Mateo's pajama pants down past his hips and began caressing his balls in time to the strokes he gave Mateo's cock. With his free hand, Mateo gripped Buckley's chin, pushing him gently backward across the kitchen floor, a slow salsa dance that ended when Buckley's bare ass hit the table's edge.

Maybe Mateo was making the story up, or embellishing it some, for Buckley's smutty benefit. Either way, he didn't care. Hell, he'd never been a pesky Mormon missionary in tight black pants, but that didn't mean he didn't love playing one face down on their living room sofa.

"What did you guys do to him?" Buckley asked in a breathless whisper.

"Second the door closed he hit his knees and started sucking our cocks. The whole two Marines at one time thing got him so hot he even sucked our dog tags. It was crazy. I'd only fooled around with a few guys, but Jeff was an expert. He taught me a lot of things that night." Mateo stroked Buckley's cock while giving him an open-mouthed kiss. "All the things I do to you I learned from Jeff."

Buckley shuddered, worried suddenly he would blow right there. And that wouldn't do because he wanted to hear the entire story.

It was like the picture of Mateo and Jeff hanging on their living room wall had come to life and taken them both back to a hot and sweaty motel room where the surf whispered outside, barely audible over the grunts and curses of men being very, very bad. The fantasy of his sweet Mateo, as buttoned-down and nervous about sex as when they'd first met, being guided in the ways of the bedroom by an experienced, confident older man was like liquid lust coursing through Buckley's veins.

"Like what?"

"The rim parade, that was him," Mateo answered. Buckley groaned. The *rim parade* was Mateo's nickname for the sequence of tongue strokes he'd first unleashed on Buckley's hole to see which one gave him the most pleasure—he'd started with long and wide, then switched to mad flickers a few seconds later, before ending with slow, wet circles that had done Buckley in. And apparently it was Jeff Braxton's nickname for it, not Mateo's.

"Twisting your nipples until you can't take it anymore." Mateo spun Buckley around and bent him forward over the kitchen table, one hand on the back of his neck, throbbing cock pressed against Buckley's hole. The strength of his erection told him that Mateo wasn't faking this for Buckley's benefit. This fantasy three-way was driving him wild as well. "It was my first time topping a guy. He gave me instructions."

"Like what?"

Mateo pressed the head of his cock against Buckley's hole. "Don't rush." Mateo replaced his cock with gently circling fingers before pressing the tip of one digit gently inside. "Warm him up, take your time."

Mateo's cock returned. He pressed it slowly inside Buckley's hole, still yielding and slick from their laundry room lovemaking. A little raw, too, but the thin edge of pain it added to the slow and steady entrance of Mateo's cock only turned Buckley on more.

"Watch the way he moves, his breaths, as you slowly slide your way in. Take your time to let him settle, adjust." Mateo increased the rhythm of his thrusts. "Jesus, *papi*. You're on fire," he added in an awestruck whisper, like a man seeing the Sistine Chapel for the first time.

"Is this how you fucked him? Is this how you fucked that twink while Jeff watched?" Buckley sounded drunk with lust, face half pressed to the kitchen table. Maybe because for the first time Mateo was pulling a fantasy out of his deepest core and not the other way around.

"Exactly how. I wanted to make him proud."

Mateo's thrusts turned hard and forceful, then long and slow. Buckley could feel himself on the verge of boiling over.

"Where was Jeff?" Buckley asked breathlessly. "Where was your crew chief while you fucked that little go-go boy?"

Silence. Had he gone too far? He hated the thought, but Mateo hadn't stopped fucking him, so maybe not.

Suddenly he felt pressure against his lips, foreign and strange. He parted them, opening his eyes to see one end of the zucchini Mateo had been chopping earlier press into his mouth. "Right here."

Buckley closed his eyes and swallowed, imagining it was another man's cock Mateo was guiding into his mouth. Not simply another man. Jeff Braxton, the mysterious master sergeant with the crystal-blue eyes. Mateo's lips met his ear. "Fucking your mouth, my sweet, beautiful slutty boy," he whispered.

Buckley couldn't remember the last time he'd come this hard—or this loud. His bellow threatened to turn into a scream. Mateo kept stroking him and fucking him in tandem, and Buckley thought the kitchen table might split from the sheer force of the pleasure roaring through his body.

He'd come out when he was fourteen and had more sexual experience with guys by the time he graduated high school than Mateo did by the time he met Buckley at age twenty-five. But whatever this was, whatever they'd just done, was *new*. It was like they'd made love across time and space and with a man he'd never met but always fantasized about. A man who held a piece of Mateo's soul in his hands. A man who was also the reason Mateo was alive today.

A door inside of Buckley had been unlocked, allowing him to feel more filled, and more emptied of all tension and strain than he'd ever felt in his life.

Opening his mouth against the back of Buckley's neck, Mateo roared loud enough to scare the neighbors, a sound so deep and powerful it suggested he'd gone to the same place Buckley had.

3

Another shower was in order. They held each other under the spray, kissing, soaping, kneading but barely speaking, as if they were amazed to have their bodies back after traveling through time astride a fantasy.

Not a fantasy, Buckley corrected himself, a memory. *A memory my boyfriend used to fill me and own me.*

A few times, he looked up, but it was hard to read Mateo's expression in the dim glow. Buckley had changed the light bulb overhead to a soft and warm one, one of many he'd installed in strategic places throughout the apartment. Dimmers were a no-go. Buckley had removed them himself. Their slow fade from light to dark was too triggering, reminding Mateo of the awful moment the Osprey had pitched forward toward the dark ocean depths after missing its landing on the aircraft carrier's deck.

An hour later, they were snuggling on the living room sofa. Haunting violin music filled their living room, but Buckley was only pretending to watch the true crime documentary they'd scrolled their way to on Netflix.

His mind was shuttling between memories of what they'd done in the kitchen and memories of what he'd done earlier that week—his last-ditch effort to get Jeff Braxton at Mateo's birthday party. Earlier, he hadn't said a word about it because if his plan worked, he wanted it to stay a surprise. Then his boyfriend had rolled out some surprises of his own. Now he wasn't sure what to do.

"Should we talk about it?" Mateo finally asked.

"Sure." Even though his heart was in his throat, he sat up slowly so he could look into Mateo's eyes.

"That was amazing, but I just want to make sure you're cool. I mean, it was a while ago."

"So it was all true?" he asked. "You guys really blew out some hot go-go boy's back?"

"You thought I made it up?"

"Parts of it, maybe. I don't know. For fun. A fantasy. Like we usually do."

Mateo caressed the side of Buckley's face. "The truth seemed to be setting you on fire, so I decided to give you more of it. That's okay, right? I mean, you said you weren't jealous, but I just want to be sure now that we…you know…"

Buckley was a fast talker. On his ambulance crews, he was usually the one tasked with calming a panicked patient with streams of focusing, comforting words. But in this moment, words failed him.

I don't get jealous when it comes to you, was what Buckley wanted to say. He somehow felt tangled up and included in Mateo's passion for other men, especially a man he worshiped. Like Mateo's lust for anyone flowed through Buckley first and with power, and this made him feel like the bond between him and Mateo was deeper than any he'd shared with another man.

"I loved it. It was like we traveled back through time together, and I got to see a different side of you."

"Alright, well," Mateo said finally, "since it looks like you're never going to meet Jeff anyway, I figure we don't have to worry about it being weird. But I wanted to be sure." Their lips met in a gentle kiss. "You sure you're cool?" he asked in a whisper.

"Cool *and* hot," Buckley whispered back. "At the same time."

"Good. But eventually," Mateo whispered, "I'm going to open up that dirty mind of yours some more. It's only fair since you've been all over mine."

He snuggled into his boyfriend's lap again.

Mateo was right.

No point getting bent out of shape over anything relating to Jeff Braxton given how hard the guy had proven to get in touch with. Maybe their kitchen session had been a fluke, and maybe the real thrill had been the sense that he was being claimed by a younger, more innocent, but no less hungry version of the man he loved.

But what if Jeff actually showed up at the party?

Should he tell Mateo about it now, just in case?

The unanswered question rattled around in his head until he fell asleep in Mateo's arms.

Days before, Buckley had given up hope of a response from Jeff Braxton, but in the wake of Mateo's big revelation, he'd spent the day leading up to the party nervously checking his texts for any message from a strange number. Crickets, except for the usual steady stream from Mateo and his sister, who was helping Buckley import elements of their old neighborhood into the celebration. The Canos could take away their support, but they couldn't take away his culture. That was the theme he and Marisol agreed on months before.

A few hours before showtime, and shortly after Buckley arrived at Sapphire Cove, prep took a turn for the worse.

Not only had the band taken the wrong exit, they were having trouble connecting to Google Maps, forcing Buckley to give them verbal directions into the resort's motor court by phone. Not the easiest thing since they were LA imports lost in the undulating labyrinth of hills between Sapphire Cove and the 405 Freeway, a place where deep canyons and a toll road could make a wrong turn into something you had to endure for twenty minutes.

Upon their delayed arrival, they realized they'd forgotten one of their amps, but the hotel's sound equipment was all in use by other events, so he'd been forced to contact a neighboring resort a short drive up the coast to find a replacement. As soon as a rental fee was agreed to, one of the guitarists rushed off to pick it up in their rattling death trap of a van.

Buckley took his first deep breath in hours.

That's when he saw he had two texts from a number he didn't recognize.

This is Jeff Braxton. I received your note. I will be there at 6:30 p.m. at the address you provided.

Then, two hours later, a second from the same number.

Here.

So Jeff had waited until the last possible second to RSVP.

How charming! Maybe he'd been deployed. But the words *the address you provided* suggested reluctance, as if he didn't want to repeat anything that might make the party sound like what it was—a classy soiree at one of the finest resorts on the Southern California coast. And the *I received your note* line made the entire invite sound like a subpoena.

What mattered was that he was at the resort right now, on the other side of the grounds from Buckley. If Buckley didn't get to him first, Mateo would when he arrived with his sister in about fifteen minutes. And then Jeff might ask him about their nonexistent move to Japan, and awkward wouldn't begin to describe it.

He took off running.

The hotel's restaurant and bar were open to the sparkling marble-floored lobby and not too crowded, but Buckley saw no sign of the mysterious Marine perched on one of its white leather stools. That's because he was walking out the automatic doors into the motor court.

Buckley raced after him. "Oh, no you don't. Stop right there, mister."

One dark eyebrow raised, assessing Buckley as if he were mildly amused the guy thought he was qualified to order him around, Jeff Braxton turned. The man's photograph only hinted at his size and power. His eyes didn't just communicate focus. In person, they blazed with intensity. As he surveyed Buckley from head to toe, Buckley felt chills move up his spine. This was the look Mateo had described, the one that could make a twink drop their undies in ten seconds flat. It made him feel like his thighs were being caressed by searching fingers.

"I brought a gift. I left it with the nice couple over there." He spoke with a controlled Texas twang that made Buckley imagine the guy throwing him across the back of a saddle.

It took him a second to realize Jeff had gestured in the direction of the bar, where Melanie Fox and her boyfriend, Tim, classmates of Mateo's from UC Irvine, were chatting over their wineglasses.

"Good night, Buckley. Enjoy whatever this is you're up to." He marched through the automatic doors.

Buckley followed him. "It's called a birthday party. And you should be here."

"Right." Cool as ice, Jeff handed his ticket to the valet. "'Cause you guys are headed to Japan in a few days? Even though Mateo's at UCI this semester and you're an EMT? Is that a thing? EMTs deploying to other countries? You know the language?"

Thanks, Melanie, Buckley thought.

"I don't look like a guy who can put in some time with Duolingo?" Buckley said.

"Maybe. What's *I'm a liar* in Japanese?"

"It sounds a lot like *you're a dick.*"

Jeff let out a low cackle as he walked closer to the edge of the curb. Buckley followed him. "Look, I'm sorry if I got sick of seeing Mateo get hurt every time he tried to reach out to you and you shut him down *again*, but Jesus, dude. Enough already. He worships you."

There was a twinge of emotion in the look Jeff gave him now, but it still made Buckley feel more like a threat the man was assessing.

"Has it ever occurred to you there's a damn good reason your boyfriend and I shouldn't be around each other?"

"I didn't know you two had history when I left the note. I thought you were straight. There's a picture of you on our wall and you looked…" *Like a hardcore daddy who could fuck me cross-eyed.*

"Old?" Jeff asked with a half smile.

"Straight."

"You're kinda out and proud to be making snap judgments based on a guy's picture."

"And where have you seen me be *out and proud* exactly?"

Jeff blushed, jaw working. "I gathered some intel when you two got together."

"You social media stalked me?"

"Mateo's one of the best guys I know. I wanted to see if you were a serial killer."

"So you're allowed to make snap judgments about people based off photographs and I'm not? Is that a Marine thing? ID'ing serial killers based on their selfies?"

The older man's amusement took the form of a small grunt in his throat, followed by a raised eyebrow. "You got a mouth on you, firecracker."

Was this the same husky tone, so close to a growl, he'd used to give Mateo instructions on how to properly fuck a guy for the first time?

All the things I do to you I learned from Jeff.

Focus, he told himself.

"When did you find out?" Jeff finally asked.

"Find out what?" Buckley hated playing dumb. He only did it when he was truly nervous, which was rare.

"That we have *history*, as you put it."

Buckley took a deep breath, fighting memories of the kitchen table turning hot against his sweating, heaving flesh, his lips parting around a vegetable turned sex toy.

Was he blushing?

It felt like he was blushing. Everywhere.

"You saved his life. I've known that from day one. But I've always wondered why you were never around. Now I know. You're really damn hard to get in touch with. And kinda a pain in the ass."

"I'm making a clean getaway before this gets weirder."

The valet approached. Buckley stepped between them and gently tugged the ticket from Jeff's hand before the valet could. Out of options, Buckley said, "His parents cut him off. Because of me."

Jeff went very still. "When?" he finally asked.

"A few months ago."

He dismissed the valet, then shook his head at the pavement, anger turning his solid body rigid. "Still taking orders from their friggin' parish priest," he muttered.

"He wants you here," Buckley said.

"Do you?" Jeff asked.

When Buckley looked up, he realized his move to intercept the ticket had left them almost face-to-face.

"*Braxton?*" A familiar voice made them both turn.

At the sight of Mateo walking toward them from the spot where his sister had handed off her Nissan Sentra to the valet, looking stunningly handsome in his dark suit and with the collar of his white dress shirt unbuttoned, a transformation overtook Jeff Braxton that was so sudden and profound Buckley found himself dazzled by the sight of it. The Marine's eyes, icy and intent a second before, became open and vulnerable. His lips parted as if he were about to speak but had forgotten the words. Fear and want combined in his expression, as if Mateo held the keys to his undoing and was dangling them in one hand.

The instant connection between both men terrified him at first. Then it washed over him, drawing him closer as they met in a fierce hug. Less of a threat and more of an invitation.

Only when Jeff's eyes met his was Mateo convinced the man was really there, standing within inches of his boyfriend, with whom he'd been exchanging tense and serious words a few seconds before. Intimate words. Like the two men shared a history he wasn't aware of, which after yesterday's kitchen session, seemed distinctly weird.

The look Jeff gave him distracted him from his paranoid suspicions. It was pure need, pure hunger. Mateo felt suddenly like he was back in that motel room in Pacific Beach, wishing his body and soul could bend to the full arc of submission the man had craved from him.

Then he was in Jeff's arms and all he could think was, *Buckley did this.*

How else to explain it?

Was it a coincidence Jeff was at Sapphire Cove the night of his party?

Had Buckley spotted him and run over to him to keep him from leaving?

Seemed farfetched, and it didn't explain the intensity of the way the two had been speaking to each other. Like co-conspirators.

"Surprise!" Buckley said.

He looked flushed and breathless and *caught*. There was no other word for it. Maybe they'd been planning a more elegant reveal than this one. But this was the same spackling of color that graced his boyfriend's skin whenever Mateo slowly, teasingly undressed him, when he kissed his thighs, when he fucked him with his fingers, tongue, heart, and soul. Somehow, Jeff had left the same pattern of blush on Buckley's cheeks and the sides of his neck.

He should be weirded out at least, suspicious at most. Instead, Mateo felt a stirring in his balls and a deep hungry ache in his gut. He found himself looking between both men as if he was trying to decipher some small, molecular trace of the currents flowing between them.

Anger. Attraction. Secrecy.

Whatever they were, they made the back of his neck tingle.

Jeff reached for the valet ticket in Buckley's hand, tugged it free, and pocketed it.

Why had Buckley been holding Jeff's ticket?

Something had happened here, and instead of pissing him off, it excited him. The idea of Jeff helping himself to Buckley's body—helping himself to *any* man Mateo had claimed—made total and perfect sense, and his ease with the prospect left him breathless and dazed. Suddenly he was imagining the two of them fucking hard and fast in some hotel room upstairs. A fantasy that should have had him punching walls and turning over the planters nearby. Instead, he was rock hard in his briefs, the fantasy as potent and powerful as the one he and Buckley had brought to life in the kitchen the day before. And instead of being upset, he was hoping Jeff had emptied himself inside of Buckley with the same thundering bellow he'd let loose when Mateo had made him come with his hand.

He doubted any of it had actually happened. But did he *want* it to be true? Was he so excited to see Jeff again that he was willing to hand over Buckley as a party favor?

Absolutely. If he could watch.

What the fuck? I'm not even drunk.

Quickly, Jeff said, "Your boyfriend here managed to track me down. I moved a few months ago."

"You did?" Mateo asked Buckley.

"I did," Buckley said, nodding. "He's your birthday surprise. Just one of them."

Jeff was a surprise. For Mateo! Even after what Mateo had revealed about their history to Buckley the day before.

Holy shit. Buckley got me a three-way for my birthday.

"Well, I can't think of a better gift." The words were out of his mouth before he could second-guess them. "Let's go in."

He curved an arm around Buckley's back and then one around Jeff's as he steered them into the lobby, his heart pounding in his chest, wondering if Buckley, the man who'd opened the door to so many of his fantasies, had set the stage for a more intense and dangerous one.

4

Jeff Braxton was a man who liked to come prepared.

Nothing had prepared him for Buckley Mitchell, not even the intel collection he'd done before deciding to accept the invite. In the photos he'd found, Mateo's boyfriend looked like a precious cupid—baby cheeks, curly blond hair, and big blue eyes that radiated innocence. He'd expected beatific smiles and batting eyelashes as a result—a submissive pretty boy who could make Mateo happy in ways Jeff couldn't, a fact that twisted Jeff's heart into knots he didn't want the world to see.

Man up, he'd told himself. Say good-bye before you lose Mateo forever.

But the Japan lie had caught him so off guard, egress seemed like the best possible response. He'd been lured there under false pretenses, most likely so Buckley could mark his territory in some embarrassing way. On his way to the motor court, he'd even checked the lobby ceiling for the stray bucket of pig's blood.

He'd never expected Mr. Mitchell to come charging after him like an aggressive thoroughbred slipping the bullpen. And those eyes. Those eyes had still blazed even after he'd been confronted with his deception. Most people hated eye contact, so Jeff always used it to disarm aggressive opponents. Buckley hadn't blinked.

And calling someone a dick not three minutes after you'd met them? He wasn't sure he'd call that *spine*, but it sure as hell took nerve.

Now, as he found himself swept inside the resort's sparkling marble lobby, Jeff felt bested. Once again, he'd underestimated a guy with a baby face, and when had that ever worked out for him?

The feel of Mateo's arm around his shoulder sent chills rising down his arms. Marisol, Mateo's sister, was lavishing them in excited descriptions of everything that awaited them inside the party. An authentic Sonoran caterer whose carne asada was to die for, a band that knew all the Mexican hits of their childhood. They even did a great rendition of Juan Gabriel's famed live performance of "Hasta Que Te Conocí."

His chest tensed. He was pretty sure that was the song that had played on Mateo's wireless speaker when he'd danced them around their motel room on that fateful night that ruined everything, their swinging hips sealed together, chills racing up Jeff's spine when the legion of trumpeters had joined in. Moments before Mateo brought his mouth to his and Jeff felt his orderly world fall away and a doorway to something forbidden and enticing open at the hands of a junior Marine he had no business dancing with, kissing with, falling into bed with.

What the hell was he doing here?

He was a forty-five-year-old man, a senior Marine with multiple combat tours, and he'd been bested by the pushy boyfriend of the man he shouldn't love.

As they walked over the thick carpeting in the corridor between ballrooms, Mateo kept looking at him, arm clamped on his shoulders, joy lighting up his big brown eyes that could always convey emotions in hypnotizing pairs—devotion and fear, desire and hurt.

Breathe, listen, survey—a time-tested strategy for breeding focus in the midst of anxiety.

He'd never been to Sapphire Cove, so he tried to ground himself by focusing on the details. White walls with glossy wainscoting, light fixtures like upended coral formations.

Suddenly Marisol threw open a set of double doors. Guests surged toward them. Some of the faces were familiar, Marines he hadn't seen in years because they'd either gotten out or been assigned to different bases. And that made it easier suddenly, that a crowd of folks rushed forward to say their hellos. Hands pumped, mildly tipsy aggressive half hugs all around. He made conversation as best he could, but Buckley Mitchell's stare was a constant presence.

It was that hug, Jeff thought. *That hug in the motor court did me in, and now I've got a target on my back.*

The ballroom had been cut in half by a divider, and almost every song the band played was in Spanish.

Mateo stayed close. The two of them told Marine stories with old friends as if no time had passed, but it felt like a performance. A good while into the party, after the birthday cake, they ended up alone together. Their high-top table was next to an open set of soaring glass doors. Outside was a narrow band of lawn and a stone balustrade. Just beyond, the cliffs plunged to what he assumed was the hotel's beach. Two glasses of champagne had dulled the edge, helping him conceal a hunger he was determined to keep hidden from the world after failing so miserably in the motor court.

Marine Corps master sergeants weren't supposed to act like lovesick teenage boys.

Because he'd been dancing with Buckley earlier, Mateo's wavy hair was rumpled, a couple black locks draping his forehead. And there was that eager look that had melted his heart so often over the years. A look that said everything they did together was an amazing adventure Jeff had made possible.

"What happened to *champagne is the cotton candy of alcohol*?" Mateo asked.

"Special occasion." Jeff toasted the birthday boy. "And I never said I hated cotton candy."

Mateo laughed, took a sip from his own sparkling flute. "You know, you can tell me if you think I wussed out. I know I didn't talk about my discharge with you before I did it…and I don't know…"

"Since when is leaving the Marines wussing out? Not everybody's cut out to be career military."

"So that's not why you went dark on me? You weren't judging me?"

"I'd never judge you."

"You judged me a little bit. Sometimes. In good ways."

"I was your staff NCO. It was my job."

Mateo smiled. "Yeah, but you also judged my surfing."

"Your surfing required work in the beginning, that's true. But as with most things in your life, it was about building up confidence through practice and routine."

But the word *surfing* took him back to that sunny afternoon on the beach at San Onofre, when he was still a gunnery sergeant and

Mateo was simply another straight Marine he was mentoring. They'd been sitting on their boards looking out at the sparkling sea when Jeff had asked him how things were going with that girl he'd been chatting with on Tinder. Out of nowhere, in a halting, unsure voice as he plucked at the cuff strap on the right ankle of his wet suit, Mateo had said, "I don't know if me and women are gonna be a thing, gunny."

And Jeff had been forced to breathe and focus like he was scanning rooftops for camouflaged snipers. Never in a million years would he have allowed himself to get so close to a Marine as sweet, innocent, and beautiful as Mateo Cano if he thought the guy had been less than a hundred percent straight, and suddenly he was stuck.

They'd had a long, careful talk that day.

Jeff was out, but he didn't skywrite it. He'd entered the Corps during the Don't Ask Don't Tell era, and some level of secrecy— what some folks liked to call *discretion*—was still wound up in his DNA. And it wasn't the first time he'd had the *When did you know for sure* talk with a young Marine who was still finding himself. But none of those guys had made his stomach somersault the way Mateo did. He was an expert at keeping his feelings for unattainable straight guys inside a box, and that's where he'd assumed his feelings for Mateo could live too. But in an instant, the way the guy always looked at him—as if he'd not only hung the moon but made it a wonderful place to live—meant something else entirely. It would take all of Jeff's strength not to explore the promise in that look, he'd realized that day.

A few months later, his strength ran out, and the result was several nights in San Diego that ruined everything.

But it sounded like Mateo hadn't even thought about their motel room antics as he'd ruminated over Jeff's retreat. Instead, the poor guy had imagined Jeff was judging him, disdaining him, when the truth was, Jeff had been feeling those things about himself.

Out on the dance floor, Marisol and another woman he didn't know made a gyrating sandwich out of Buckley. Crazy thoughts surged through his head at the sight of his swinging hips. Mateo's hands gripping them. Jeff's hands caught up in Mateo's. Borders blurred, rules broken.

What would it be like to watch Mateo plow that firecracker hard?

Wishful thinking, assuming he'd been brought here as some sort of birthday hookup.

Buckley was probably pissed as hell, which was why he was steering clear of them now. He'd tried to surprise his boyfriend with his long-lost friend only to find out the two of them had hooked up. And because Jeff had been a giant wuss about texting back, he hadn't given Buckley an opportunity to share his feelings about the revelation and politely ask him not to show. The most plausible storyline for this wildly messed-up evening, he was sure.

And if every now and then Buckley shot them both a searching look that seemed a little mischievous, he was probably strategizing on how to embarrass Jeff without ruining Mateo's party. Just like Jeff was trying to figure out how to expose Buckley's lie about moving to Japan without killing the celebration.

"So Buckley said something happened with your parents."

Mateo winced. Jeff tried not to wince too, regretting the curveball he'd thrown. He'd wanted to show concern, but he'd also used a painful subject to deflect from his dark plotting.

"Father Jones strikes again. Soon as I told them I had a boyfriend, they went to Jones to talk about it. He said if they allowed me to bring Buckley this Christmas, they were violating God's will for me. I don't even think they really believe it. They just worship the guy more than Jesus. He was there for them and all of their friends when they first came to America, so the bond is…intense."

"So they told you Buckley couldn't come to the house and then what?"

"I said it was either both of us or neither of us."

Jeff was stunned. And impressed. The Mateo of two years ago lived in mortal fear of disappointing his mom and dad.

"Good for you, man," Jeff said.

"Buckley's worth it."

But there was heartbreak in his eyes. Mateo lived for Christmas. Whenever he'd told stories about all the decorations he'd plaster all over his parents' house, he'd turn bright-eyed and boyish, earning a fair amount of ribbing from his fellow Marines. *Padre Navidad*, they'd called him. And Mateo had accepted the title proudly.

"He's what you need."

Mateo looked to his boyfriend. "So when did you guys connect? I mean, how'd he find you? 'Cause you didn't exactly make it easy."

Might as well cut right to it, Jeff thought. "I didn't want to get in the way."

"Of college?" Mateo asked.

"Of Buckley. You and Buckley."

There, I fucking said it. If he doesn't know how bad I ache for him after that, I've got no other way to say it.

"I don't think he would have let you." Mateo's eyes found his dancing boyfriend. "Buckley's unstoppable."

He was looking at the man in question the way he'd just looked at Jeff. Like he'd followed a cord of desire connecting them both, and the desire he felt for the man at each end was equal.

"So he knows," Jeff said, and Mateo looked back at him. "About San Diego. You and me…"

Mateo nodded. He seemed distant and lost in thought, the same way he had during his Marine Corps days when he was trying to work up the nerve to overcome his fears.

"When did you tell him?"

"Yesterday."

Which meant the guy had barely had time to recover. And given Jeff's radio silence after the initial invite, he'd probably assumed he wasn't coming and it wouldn't be an issue. Sure, it would have been ballsy for Buckley to write back into that void, asking Jeff not to come after all. But he'd already nicknamed the guy firecracker based on his smart mouth, so could Jeff really put it past him? Mateo looked like he was processing this information as well.

"Did you guys meet? Like, in person?" Mateo sounded so tense, he might as well have asked him if they'd hooked up.

"He slipped a note under my door with his phone number."

Mateo was smiling into his drink suddenly.

"What?" Jeff asked.

"For a second there out front I thought maybe you guys had history too," Mateo said, then stole a quick sip of champagne.

Well, there's this story about Japan, but Jeff didn't want to go there yet so he changed subjects. "How did it come up?" he said instead. "You know, you and me in Pacific Beach and what's his name?"

Heart racing, Jeff was back in that motel room again. Watching the joy come into Mateo's eyes as he'd pounded that hungry little dancer, then the eagerness in his expression when he'd looked to him for approval, and Jeff had responded in the only way he could, with their first deep, devouring kiss.

Mateo's easy smile made Jeff go soft in some places and hard in others, all places he should be rushing to armor as he headed for the exit.

The first night of the trip had been a fantasy made real. On the last night, everything had fallen apart, but they'd pretended otherwise. That's when Jeff had unleashed his dominant desires and beneath him Mateo had stiffened with resistance, a terrible moment of understanding, a recognition of deep, primal incompatibility, followed by a look of disappointment on Mateo's face when he realized he couldn't give Jeff everything he wanted. And Jeff had backed off, assuming with dread in his gut and a terrible ache in his heart, that he'd ended their friendship by reaching too far and too fast for something that wasn't his to claim. Worse, he'd assumed that if he'd pressed harder, Mateo might have given him something he didn't want to give, and the prospect hurt him like a bullet in his gut.

Mateo carefully sipped his drink. "I sent you an invite, a card. It got returned. When I saw it in the mail I told him it was probably…"

"Probably what?"

"For the better. That you didn't come. Given our history."

Jeff's heart was in his throat. "Still feel that way?"

Mateo's eyes met his. "Hell, no. Didn't feel that way then. It just seemed like something to say. I was upset. He could tell. And he knows who you are, obviously. I've got a picture of you on my wall. You and me, I mean."

Jeff tried not to blush. He'd been having the same thought about that photo ever since Buckley had mentioned it. It was another sign Mateo didn't think of those nights back in San Diego the way Jeff did. With remorse and threads of shame woven through them.

"I missed you," Mateo said. "It hurt, how much I missed you."

Suddenly there was no music, no other guests. Just those big, pleading brown eyes and that earnest soul, older and more mature now. More comfortable in his skin. More intoxicating and hypnotic. More aware of what he wanted. And right now, even with his boyfriend dancing a few feet away, what he wanted seemed to be Jeff.

"So what'd you get me?" Mateo asked. "For my birthday?"

"It's over on the gift table. I'll grab it."

He was grateful for the chance to pull away from the seductive power of Mateo's gaze, but he'd barely taken a step before the man seized his wrist in a powerful grip. "I've got a better idea."

They were face-to-face, noses almost touching. They hadn't been this close since that night.

"Go dance with my boyfriend."

For a second, he thought the request was Mateo's way of defusing the tension between his old mentor and the man he loved. But Mateo hadn't seen that tension in action. What he was asking for, and the hungry way he'd asked for it, seemed like something altogether more complicated. But there was unsteadiness in his voice, too, a bit of fear, as if he was trying to make himself comfortable with the thought of Jeff and Buckley dancing together.

Jeff was about to protest. He didn't dance to fast songs, and Buckley was surrounded. Then the band launched into a slow rendition of "Bésame Mucho," and half the dance floor either coupled up or cleared out, leaving a clean path between him and Buckley, who was staring at him with a look in his eyes that seemed as hungry as the one in Mateo's.

5

Jeff started for Buckley across the dance floor, reminding himself he'd faced down far more formidable opponents in his life, some of them armed. A close slow dance didn't have to be awkward or tense. It could be a perfect opportunity to talk some quiet, forceful sense into the situation.

He'd apologize for hurting Mateo with his radio silence, but he'd also make clear he had every intention of telling the guy about Buckley's lie. All in a reasonable, mature tone, the kind he used with his junior Marines. And he'd do it pronto, establishing dominance before the dangerous cupid could unleash that wicked little mouth on him. Again.

But when he took Buckley's hand, looked into those big, beautiful eyes that seemed to smile even when his bow-shaped lips didn't, all that came out was, "Where'd you find the band, firecracker?"

"Marisol did. They're old friends of theirs from Huntington Park. Most of them have regular gigs playing backup for big musicians so they get together on the weekends and do the songs they grew up with." The drowsy, lilting love song seemed to wrap its gently swaying arms around them both, and Jeff felt himself being seduced into forgetting his complaints about the evening entirely. But it was Buckley who broke the silence. "His parents can take away their support, but they can't take away his culture. That's the theme for the evening, basically."

The statement's sincerity and quiet force tugged at him, proved

Buckley Mitchell could use his determination and smarts for something other than deception. The idea of someone else doing such a good job of loving Mateo, *protecting* Mateo, warmed his heart. What that said about his love for the guy felt as complicated as everything else about this night.

He was supposed to be putting the kid back in his place after their sparring session in the motor court, but Buckley's cologne was citrusy and slightly sweet, and his half smile carried the seductive power of an embrace. When Jeff looked into his blue eyes, he felt like a sailor heeding the call of a siren. This particular rendition was one of the slowest, most lilting versions of "Bésame Mucho" he'd ever heard.

"Question, firecracker. What was your plan once I found out you lied to get me here?"

He didn't flinch. "I was going to meet you at the front door and give you a piece of my mind first. I figured by then you'd be too shamed to object."

"Gotcha. Well, I'm telling him what you did."

Buckley's smile grew. "But you haven't yet."

"I'll tell him after, when there aren't so many guests around."

"So you're having a terrible time and you hated seeing him again and you wish you hadn't come and that talk you had over there was the worst thing you've ever experienced even though you were both grinning and laughing like schoolboys."

Jeff felt himself blush. "A lie's a lie."

"I see. The hotel threw in a villa for the weekend. Tell him there. After. In case he gets upset. Which he won't. Because you're here, and that's what he wanted." Like it was nothing, inviting him back to their romantic hotel suite. Maybe it was nothing. And the truth was, he didn't want to ruin Mateo's party.

"I'll have champagne ready just in case," Buckley added.

"His idea, by the way," Jeff said. "That I dance with you, I mean."

"And you're only doing it to make him happy, is that it?"

"Basically."

As if this were a respectful answer, Buckley nodded.

When he shot a look in Mateo's direction, Jeff followed suit.

The expression on Mateo's face caught him off guard, maybe because like so many other things about the man he'd encountered that night it was the product of a Mateo who was infinitely more comfortable in his skin than the one he'd first met. Back then, he'd been bashful to a fault. Off base, when he wasn't standing at attention, he'd bow his head and smile nervously whenever he was uncomfortable, which was a lot. Under Jeff's strategic bursts of eye contact, he'd usually blush and fold, but for most of the evening he'd been meeting Jeff's looks head on, returning them with expressions ranging from the joyful to the wounded to the…

How exactly to describe the way he was looking at him now? Leaning forward, elbows resting on the high-top table, watching the two of them with unguarded hunger.

Both of us, Jeff realized. *He's looking at* both *of us like that.*

"Well, good," Buckley said. "Tonight is about making Mateo happy."

"I get it. So you're that kind of guy," Jeff said.

"*What* kind of guy is that?"

"The kind who puts everyone else's needs ahead of their own."

Buckley cocked one eyebrow. "Pretty big assumption coming from someone who avoided getting to know me for a year."

"Yeah, well, it usually means one thing."

"Which is?"

Realizing he'd nervously looked away, Jeff returned his gaze to Buckley. "You're afraid to admit what you want."

"And what do I want, Master Sergeant Braxton?"

"You want to answer questions with questions, apparently."

Buckley smiled. "You don't ask questions. You make announcements. And give orders."

"Why didn't you call me and ask me not to come after you found out about us?"

Buckley's smile got bigger. "Because I'm not sixteen."

The scathing accuracy of the answer left Jeff's mouth dry.

"Or it was a *keep your friends close but your enemies closer* kind of thing."

Buckley's slow nod seemed like a mask over a deeper, possibly painful, reaction, but he didn't seem all that upset. This was definitely the guy you wanted holding your hand in the ambulance after you'd broken both legs.

"So you're my enemy?" Buckley finally asked.

"Competition, maybe. Or you think so. And you're wrong."

"Since we're doling out assumptions here, I'm going to go ahead and say I think you believe the worst of everyone because it makes you feel like you're in control."

"Trust me, I've got no illusions about controlling you, firecracker. Mateo says you're unstoppable, and I believe him."

"When I think something's the right thing for someone. For someone I love. That's why I spent a week trying to find your new address."

"What's the right thing for *you* though?"

"I love him more than anyone I've ever known, and his life isn't complete without you. So I want you in it. Regardless of the risks."

What risks was he referring to, especially since he'd just said he didn't consider Jeff his competition? He wasn't about to ask. Describing the risks might make him more susceptible to them.

"You know, this is one of his favorite songs," Buckley said. "Consuelo Velázquez wrote it before she'd ever kissed anyone. She was twenty. When they asked her how she came up with it, she called it a product of her imagination. He used to play it in his room when he was a kid and imagine kissing other boys. He calls it his Consuelo Velázquez era."

"How'd you two meet?" Jeff asked.

"Dating app."

"Sweet. Traditional."

Buckley laughed. "What, you thought I met him dancing on a bar?"

"I don't know. You've certainly got the moves for it."

"Thank you. I guess."

"The moves he needs, anyway."

"So he doesn't get to have the man he worships in his life because he couldn't bottom for you?"

"Watch your step, firecracker."

Buckley squeezed Jeff's palm and smiled. "I'm leading, if you haven't noticed," he whispered.

"I'll tell you what I just told him. I didn't want to get in the way."

"I see. So you think you're *my* competition?"

"Before you were in play, there was a serious risk of Mateo giving me something he didn't want to give 'cause he knew how bad I wanted it. I didn't want him doing that. To himself or to me. That's what I think."

"So when it comes to him, we're both martyrs, is that it?"

"I prefer *mature*."

"Uh-huh. So turning your back on someone you love because you can't own their ass is *mature*."

"Lying to get what you want isn't exactly what I'd call adult."

They'd ended up back where they'd started this evening, but Buckley seemed delighted to be there again, and damn if Jeff didn't feel a powerful heat in the hand with which he gripped Buckley's, damn if he didn't find it impossible to look away from the twinkle of a mischievous smile in Buckley's stare. Damn if it didn't thrill him to think about the sweaty and passionate hours this strutting, confident man had spent drawing out the flirty, comfortable, self-assured version of Mateo he'd fallen in love with all over again that night.

He couldn't decide if he wanted to turn Buckley Mitchell over his knee or taste him from head to toe, and he was starting to suspect if he put the decision to Buckley, the guy would say, *Why choose?*

"Lawyers for parents, right?" Jeff said. "You're good at interrogations. Both sides of them."

"My dad sold a tech company he started when I was a baby. My mom was his business affairs person. They were retired as long as I remember. Mostly they partied and traveled."

"Gotcha. So raised by one lawyer, and you put people back together for a living. Sounds like you were the only adult in the house growing up."

"That's fair. And you?"

"Only lawyers my family ever dealt with were public defenders. I raised my little sister. Our parents weren't really in the picture."

"How'd that go?"

He hoped the memory stabbing him in the gut didn't show on his face—he and his baby sister standing on the front porch of their old double-wide, their uncle pacing furiously before them as a dark realization set in. It wasn't the first time their parents had gone off on a bender. But it was the first time they'd been gone more than two weeks. And how did their uncle react once he realized he had no choice but to take in his alcoholic brother's kids? Blamed them for their parents' addiction, that's what. *If you kids hadn't been so much stress*, he'd said through clenched teeth, *they wouldn't have run off like this.* Forty plus years later, Jeff tried to breathe through the memory of the most stable person in his family accusing him and his sister of destroying their family through the crime of being six and seven years old.

It didn't take a therapist to see why Jeff struggled to feel like he belonged in any place where he wasn't given a specific rank along with a manual outlining standard operating procedures. And boy, was this night lacking in both.

"She's a doctor today at Parkland, so I'd say, well enough."

Buckley nodded, studying him as if he'd sensed the memory moving through him like a dark but fast-moving cloud. "You certainly did a good job with Mateo," he finally said, softly, as if he wanted the words to be a comfort to a man clearly fighting pain.

"He's not my child."

"You know what I mean."

"Thank you. But I'm still telling him you lied to get me here."

He felt an arm curve around his shoulders, thought for a second that Buckley had grown a third one, then realized Mateo was enfolding them both in a wide embrace as he crooned the last words of the song. Then he kissed them both on the cheek and tried to ruffle Jeff's close-cropped hair with one hand, but his hair was so short the gesture turned into a rough rub that sent delicious chills coursing down Jeff's back. The same response Jeff had whenever Mateo touched him. Crazy thing was he was getting it from Buckley's grip now too.

But Mateo's expression showed that same mix of fear and excitement Jeff had heard in the guy's voice when he'd asked Jeff to slow dance with Buckley.

Buckley said, "Jeff's going to come back to the villa with us after and hang out for a bit. He has something super important to tell you." Buckley rolled his eyes so hard Jeff thought about smacking him on the butt. "I'm going to go hand out some tip money and start wrapping things up. It's 6E in case anyone gets lost. Try to hold off on the big revelation until I get back."

Then Buckley was gone, and Jeff was trying to forget the villa number as hard as he could, even as it carved itself into his memory.

6

On the southern edge of Sapphire Cove's promontory, the resort's private villas were accessed by sloping stone staircases that traveled downhill between each row. As they waited for Buckley, Mateo pretended to listen to the story Jeff was telling him about an old Marine Corps buddy of theirs, a straight guy who had deluded himself into believing that most of the subscribers who watched the naked workout videos he posted on his OnlyFans page were female.

While he laughed in all the right places, he only heard every other word.

I can do this, he thought, over and over again. We *can do this*.

But his pulse was roaring in his ears. He tried to stop himself from playing with the collar of his shirt. It wasn't that tight, and he wasn't wearing a tie. No doubt Jeff's big revelation was going to be that Buckley had brought him in for a surprise three-way. He couldn't work up the nerve to ask him about it while they were alone. But if that was the case, why had Buckley rolled his eyes before walking off? There were parts about this night that weren't making a lot of sense, but maybe that's how you always felt when you were about to try something new and naked. With the two men you loved more than anyone.

For the entire party, he'd been working up the nerve to get to this moment, and as he'd watched them dance together, felt waves of desire turn his first flare of jealousy into something deeper and more powerful and hungrier, he'd convinced himself he was ready. Now, standing in the shadows with the man who'd saved his life, the man he thought he'd lost forever, he wasn't so sure.

Maybe some more champagne would help.

When they heard Buckley approaching, both of them stood up straight.

Buckley must have been nervous too. He avoided both of their stares as he opened the villa's door with his key card.

Inside, the lights had already been dimmed. Battery-operated pillar candles flickered on most of the surfaces. The deck door had been left open. Beyond the fluttering drapes and the compact terrace, the coastline to the south twinkled, the lights pouring out of the night-dark hills like little rivers of golden magma. A champagne bucket rested in the center of the sitting room's coffee table. An intimate evening for two had just added a special guest.

The beauty of the room flushed his nerves away.

"Papi." He pulled Buckley close from behind and kissed him gently on the back of the neck. "This is amazing. We get to spend all weekend here?"

Before Buckley answered, Jeff said, "You two pour a glass and sit. We need to get some stuff on the table."

"Desserts?" Buckley asked.

The master sergeant answered by closing the villa's door behind him firmly, then he gestured to the chaise lounge.

Buckley went for the bottle and poured both flutes. There was another pair on the wet bar in the corner of the room.

"You're not having one?" he asked.

"I'm good," Jeff answered.

Buckley handed Mateo a glass. Then they both did as the older man had instructed, sinking to the chaise with their backs to the open door and its beautiful view. As Jeff approached them both, Mateo slid one hand across Buckley's thigh protectively, but in his mind's eye he was already opening Buckley's legs farther so Jeff could sink to his knees before prying Buckley from his dress pants.

"Alright—" Jeff began.

"Yes!" Mateo said before he could stop himself.

And then nobody said anything. Maybe because Mateo's voice had come out like a high bark with a tremor in it.

Mateo swallowed. "Yes," he said. "Let's do it."

"Do what?" Buckley asked softly.

"I…"

Mateo's cheeks pulsed. He struggled for breath. Buckley turned to him quickly, curving an arm around his back. All of a sudden, Mateo felt like the ground was falling out from under him and he could feel his forehead sinking into his upturned palms without remembering he'd lifted his hands from his lap and Buckley's.

"Babe, what?" Buckley asked softly.

"I thought…" Swallowing again only made his throat feel dryer. "You said he was my surprise…I thought we were gonna…"

Jeff put his hands up. "And on that note, I'm outta here."

"Park it, Master Sergeant!" Buckley snapped, trigger finger pointed at the guy. "Your radio silence caused this weirdness, so you stay right there until we've figured this out."

"Fine, then," Jeff said. "But I'm laying it all out on the table. One, I was a shit to go dark on you the way I did, Cano. I should have been clear with you about what was going on. But what's clear now is this. You need someone like Buckley. Someone who can give you what you want. And I gotta say, I like this version of you a lot. I know the deal with your parents hurts, but you're happy. I can see it. And you're happy because of him."

To Buckley, he said, "And you, mouthy little fuck that you are, you're a good influence on him. He's more confident. He's more comfortable in his skin. He's loving his life. Because of you. But this role of yours, it comes with responsibility. The responsibility to be truthful. And honest."

Buckley rolled his eyes. "Fire away, big man."

Jeff turned his full attention to Mateo, whose head was still spinning from how badly he'd misread the evening. "Your boyfriend lied to get me here tonight. He slid a note under my door saying you guys were moving to Japan for work and he had no idea when you'd be back."

Mateo summoned the nerve to look his boyfriend in the eye. "Japan?"

"I had to pick somewhere far."

"We don't speak Japanese."

"Mexico's too close."

A few feet away, Jeff cleared his throat.

Buckley smiled. "Clearly that didn't go the way you'd planned, Master Sergeant. Gotta plan B? Or a lecture B? Maybe you could use PowerPoint this time."

"It went perfectly. Everything's out in the open now. You know our history, and Mateo knows about the lie you told." He made a dusting motion with both hands that was answered with brittle silence.

Mateo finally found his voice. "You did that for me? Just to get him here?"

Buckley nodded. "I knew how badly you wanted to see him. I could feel it."

Buckley rubbed Mateo's back, and for a second, Mateo thought they might be able to let the whole misunderstanding roll by. But it hadn't simply been a misunderstanding. It had turned into a want, a need, and it was still with him.

"That's the only reason you wanted him to come?" Mateo asked. "Even after yesterday?"

Buckley caressed the side of Mateo's face. "Babe, I would never ambush you like that."

"What happened yesterday?" Jeff asked.

"He told me about Pacific Beach." Buckley was still staring into Mateo's eyes, but his look had turned intense.

"What happened in Pacific Beach?" Jeff asked.

"Oh my God. Are you really playing dumb right now?" Buckley asked him.

Jeff's eyes blazed. "I know what *I* think happened in PB. I want to hear what *Mateo* thinks happened in PB."

"You first," Mateo said.

Jeff nodded confidently, but his puckered lips and tense jaw made it clear he was struggling with his next words. "I ruined our friendship, that's what happened."

"Nothing that happened in that room was as bad as you going dark on me. And our friendship's not ruined." Jeff nodded, studied the floor between them. "And it was more than friendship and you know it."

Jeff looked up as if a gun had gone off. Mateo was terrified of what he'd said, terrified it would make Buckley run from the room with tears in his eyes. But his boyfriend continued to hold him close.

"You've got a boyfriend. A good one. One who's right for you. That's what matters now."

"You're right," Mateo said, "and all night I've been thinking about you fucking him."

He'd meant it to sound like a painful confession of his stupidity, of how badly he'd misread the night's events, but instead the words came from him with more confidence than any he'd spoken since the three of them had stepped into this beautiful, candlelit villa together.

"Babe," Buckley whispered.

"I'm sorry. I've been trying to work up the nerve for it all night 'cause I thought it was the surprise, so I'm a little off center, I guess."

"A three-way with Jeff?" Buckley asked. "Babe, that's not something I'd...*ambush* you with. I mean, we haven't done anything with anyone else since we got together. I'd talk to you first. We'd talk about rules and boundaries and what we're comfortable with. You really think I'd surprise you with something that big?"

Mateo managed a smile. "He's not *that* big."

"Shut up, dude. I'm huge." Jeff's grin was soft, but it was sincere.

Buckley cleared his throat. "Seriously, babe. This is important to me. I need you to know that I'd never just throw something like that at you without warning. Did you really think I'd do that?"

"I don't know. You're...you're so much more experienced than me in this area. Everything you've suggested we do in the bedroom has been kind of amazing. So I figured if I just went along with it, it would be great. Kinda like the kitchen yesterday."

"The kitchen?" Jeff asked.

Buckley gave him a pointed look. "Don't ask questions you don't want answers to."

"I don't. What happened in the kitchen?" Jeff repeated.

"When I told him about our little PB excursion, he didn't get mad. He got turned on. So we kinda relived it. Only the part of that go-go boy was played by Buckley Mitchell. And the part of Jeff Braxton was played by..."

"A zucchini," Buckley answered.

"You couldn't find a cucumber?"

"It wasn't exactly planned, alright?" Mateo said. "I had to make do with what I was cooking."

Jeff looked back and forth between the two of them. He'd gone still and focused, the same way he had on patrol when his spider senses had told him unwanted company was near. And it took Mateo a second to realize Jeff was riveted by Buckley, by how his nostrils were flaring from his struggle to breathe deeply, how he was staring down at his lap as if he might find words of wisdom there.

Buckley was the one who'd told Jeff not to leave. Maybe he was waiting for a signal. Or maybe he was looking for something else, something that made Mateo's heart start to race again. Not permission to leave. Permission to start something else, something that wasn't merely role-play and memory. Something that might change their lives forever, starting here, in this room.

"Mateo, what do you say we grab lunch next weekend? We can meet halfway. Carlsbad, Oceanside. Reset and…"

The sound of Buckley's wet sniffle startled them both. He was crying.

Mateo caressed the side of Buckley's face, used the gesture to gently bring Buckley's attention up from his lap. "What is it, *papi*?"

"I keep trying to be jealous of you two and it keeps turning into something else before I can stop it."

"What?"

Buckley shook his head. "I always thought I would change when I fell in love. That whoever that guy was, I'd want to own him completely. Be their number one. But then I found you and I loved you more than anything, and I realized my idea of being someone's number one is different than most people's."

"Different how?" Mateo asked.

"I want you to have what you want, Mateo. No. It's more than that. It's…you getting what you want turns me the fuck on. The thought of you with someone else is as hot for me as if you'd touched me yourself. It's not just a don't ask, don't tell thing. It's like we're connected. You're the center of my desire, and when you get fed, I get fed."

"Is this why role-play days are always about me?" he asked.

Buckley nodded into Mateo's chest. "Yes. I mean, banging the delivery boy's one thing. But this felt, like, next level. Are you going to leave me?"

"Because you get turned on by the thought of me with other guys? Hell, no."

Jeff cleared his throat. "Alright, drama queens. Come in for a landing already. The champagne's been flowing. It's been a long night. Relax and rejoin reality already."

Slipping free of Mateo's embrace, Buckley started for the master sergeant with anger in his step. "Which feeling of mine are you dismissing, exactly?"

"Aw, God. Millennials and their feelings," Jeff growled.

"Yeah, running from yours went great, Boomer."

Jeff's eyes blazed. "I'm Gen X, smart mouth."

As Mateo walked up to them both, Buckley looked like he was in danger of hurling himself fists first against Jeff Braxton's broad, muscular chest.

His expression must have frightened the man because he raised his hands in front of him as Buckley took another few steps closer. "You two ever watch porn together?" Jeff asked, suddenly sounding like Mr. Reasonable.

"What does that have to do with anything?" Buckley asked.

"Nothing wrong with it. It can just put ideas in your head, is all. Make you think you're into stuff you're not really into. I mean, have you ever thought about what it would really feel like to have the entire soccer team run a train on you? You'd be in the hospital for a week."

"I don't need a top lecturing me on bottom fantasies. And I don't need *you* lecturing me at all. But I'm starting to think you lecture the floor before you walk on it."

"Hilarious."

"Not for the floor. It's probably sick of listening to you." In his best Jeff Braxton impression, Buckley said, "Point A. Stay completely flat while I'm on top of you or there will be consequences for every board here."

"*Guys.*" Mateo struggled to contain his laughter.

When he gripped the back of Buckley's neck, Mateo told himself he was doing it to keep his boyfriend from springing on his best friend, but then he felt the man he loved go limp under his touch. "Come on. Let's work this out," he whispered.

"Your boyfriend's impossible," Jeff whispered, but he didn't sound angry or firm. He sounded awestruck. "Fucking impossible."

"Your old crew chief's a jerk," Buckley whispered back.

Jeff huffed with laughter at the lameness of the comeback.

With a confident grip, Mateo gently massaged the back of Buckley's neck. Then he reached up and grabbed the back of Jeff's neck too.

"Yeah, sure," Mateo said softly. "You two just can't stand each other, right? Well, let's work it out. Together. That's what I want for my birthday."

It was now or never, he thought.

Gently, he brought their mouths together, felt his skin catch fire at the sight of the men he loved parting their lips in the instant before those same lips met with sudden, hungry force.

Buckley's knees went weak from the white-hot wrongness of kissing another man for the first time in a little over a year, a full-body reaction that sent a pulse from his toes to his head. Like touching a stove that should have been hot but instead felt like soft velvet. The lips were not Mateo's. They were rougher, the kisses more forceful. But that initial sense of having broken some vow was melted by the kneading, insistent force Mateo was applying to the back of their necks.

In the blink of an eye, with a single gesture, Mateo had closed the distance between Buckley and Jeff, and before Buckley realized what had happened, the feel of Jeff's lips against his had seized control of him.

And then the kiss caught fire, and he found himself thrilling over the taste of Jeff's tongue as the man's big, gym-calloused hands caressed the side of his face. His boyfriend let out a gentle, satisfied groan even though it was Jeff's mouth Buckley was tasting. The Marine kissed like Mateo kissed, with a steady, probing build. That and the way Buckley went up on the balls of his feet to take in more of the man's hungry mouth gave a raw, hot truth to the lie that had been their anger a second before.

"There we go," Mateo whispered next to them. "That's it. That's what you guys need." His voice made it sound like some deep knot of tension had been released from his own body, even though he wasn't being touched.

At this added burst of permission, Buckley leaned into Jeff's hungry, forbidden kiss. Suddenly his hands were resting against the man's chest, and he was feeling the hard plates of muscle there that had been off limits only a short while before.

"Wicked mouth." It took a second for Buckley to realize it was Jeff who'd whispered this. "God, you got a wicked, beautiful mouth."

This dazed-sounding expression of desire coming so quickly on the heels of his pompous lectures made Buckley's head spin. Right under the surface of Jeff Braxton's hard, commanding shell was a storm of desires preparing to sweep Buckley off his feet.

When he caught his breath, he saw the angry intensity that had filled Jeff's eyes for most of the night had been replaced by hard focus softened by desire. A desire Mateo had unleashed with soft, encouraging words and gently guiding hands.

Buckley went to kiss his boyfriend, only to be stopped with a hand in the center of his chest. "Nope. You two clearly have something to work out first." Mateo took a step back and slowly sank to a seat on the chaise lounge, giving them center stage.

"You sure about this, Cano?" Jeff asked, but he was studying Buckley's face like he was planning the map of his next kiss.

"Of course I'm sure. Happy birthday to me."

Buckley searched Mateo for any sign he was lying about his feelings, forcing himself to do something he didn't want to so he could make one of Buckley's fantasies come true. But his boyfriend was watching them in the same way he'd watched them dance, with a hungry half smile that had only flitted occasionally across his face when they first started seeing each other, and which had become a staple of his regular expressions ever since he'd opened up about his deepest desires.

"Buckley," Mateo said, "I want you to tell me what you used to think about whenever you looked at the picture of Jeff on our wall."

"I thought about—"

"Nope," Mateo said, one finger raised. "Look into his eyes while you say it."

Buckley swallowed and obeyed. Heat jolted up his spine when he saw the strength with which Jeff looked back.

"I thought about him fucking me."

"Aw, come on, *papi*. I know you can be more specific than that. You've got a dirty imagination. We've been using it for a year."

His chest rising slowly from a strained breath, Buckley looked into Jeff's eyes. "I thought about staring up into his eyes while he fucked me. And then…"

"And then?"

"You holding me. Under me while he fucks me and then… You're inside me too."

"Too?" Mateo asked. "Both of us? Inside you? At the same time?"

Throat dry, Buckley nodded.

Jeff's voice broke the silence. "Ever taken two men at the same time, firecracker?"

"I could learn."

A silence settled over the room. Maybe it was a shocked one, but from the blazing intensity in Jeff's and Mateo's expressions, it seemed more like a beast living inside each man had been brought to its feet by the smell of fresh bait. The prospect of owning Buckley's ass—together.

A soft, tugging sound drew his attention. Mateo had unzipped his suit pants and released his ragingly hard cock. Another signal this was turning into exactly the birthday present he wanted.

"Your turn, Master Sergeant," Mateo said. "What were you really thinking about when you danced with my boyfriend tonight?"

Jeff studied Buckley for what felt like an eternity. Mateo leisurely stroked himself as he waited for him to answer.

Slowly, the older man reached up and cupped the side of his face in one hand. "I wanted to know if these lips taste as good as they look."

"Good," Mateo said. "We're making progress. What else?"

"I wanted to make a meal out of him with you the way we did that go-go boy."

Mateo closed his eyes briefly. He drew his hand back. Buckley knew that look. It was the look he made when he was about to blow too soon. Steadying himself with a deep breath, Mateo said, "Let's see what kind of meal you make out of him first."

"Any tips?"

"From me? You taught me everything I know, Master Sergeant."

Rising to his feet, eyes lust hooded, Mateo watched them closely as he removed his jacket and set it on the chaise beside him. He unbuckled his belt and pushed his pants down to the floor.

Buckley prepared for his advance, expecting his boyfriend to join them, but Mateo, half naked now and throbbing with evidence of his arousal, sank back down to a seat on the chaise, content to watch, looking utterly confident and in control of the scene before him. Somehow this made Buckley feel more deliciously dominated than when Mateo was deep inside of him and pinning him to the mattress.

Buckley's jacket was sliding off of him, too, but it was Jeff who was removing it. "You know this one well, though. You've been learning his body for a year." After he tossed Buckley's jacket to the floor, he went after the buttons on his shirt, slowly, methodically. Gazing down at the Marine's working hand Buckley gasped at the occasional brush of the man's fingers against his bare skin.

"I'll tell you this, Master Sergeant. He likes a gentleman in the streets and a filthy pig in the sheets. And when he's on his knees, he is one dirty, hungry slut."

He'd never had a hands-free orgasm in his life, and certainly never jetted inside of his pants from nothing other than heated dirty talk. Another few seconds of this and both possibilities might become reality. When Jeff brought their lips together again, this time adding a firm grip to the back of his neck, Buckley felt even closer to an eruption.

"That's good," Jeff said, nostrils flaring when they broke for breath. "That's real good. On your fucking knees, firecracker. Make your boyfriend proud."

<h1 style="text-align:center">7</h1>

Christmas Eve, when he knew his parents had gotten him that Xbox he'd been begging for. The first night in his own bed after a long deployment. These moments had filled him with almost as much delicious anticipation as the sight of his boyfriend kneeling before the man who'd saved his life.

Gently, tenderly, Buckley fished Jeff's cock from his suit pants, taking a moment to marvel, wide-eyed, over its throbbing length. Realizing, no doubt, that he was about to savor its once forbidden pleasure with permission. Jeff cupped the back of his head, trying not to force the younger man's mouth into action before he was ready, clearly struggling to be worshiped when he was desperate to claim and devour.

Then Buckley gave Mateo an eager, silent look. Mateo nodded. The simple gesture made him feel more powerful than surviving boot camp without a broken bone. In an instant that stole Mateo's breath and turned the sides of his face hot, Buckley swallowed Jeff's cock, eyes locked with Mateo's the whole time.

Once again, he had to pull his hand back from his absent stroking. He wanted to edge his way through every second of this, and he'd been wholly unprepared for the ball-tensing, full-body response he'd get watching Buckley with another man for the first time.

Not just any other man. Jeff.

He was feeling the very thing Buckley had described moments earlier. Buckley was getting fed, and so Mateo was getting fed too. Meanwhile, from the looks of it, Jeff was getting one of the best blow jobs he'd ever gotten in his life. More importantly, Buckley's fantasies were also being revealed for the first time. Fantasies of serving, performing, and taking direction. Of being watched and directed and guided. And shared.

"Christ," Jeff whispered, nearly breathless with pleasure.

Knowing his boyfriend liked his sex talk dirty and porny to the extreme, Mateo decided to steer them into that line. "Got myself an A-plus cocksucker, didn't I, Master Sergeant?"

Jeff's face lit up with a smile, but he swallowed quickly. "Sure did, Cano. You sure did." He was clearly struggling to play along thanks to the incapacitating pleasure, but the dialogue was authentic and accurate. Buckley was amazingly skilled in this area, and the first time he'd gone to work on Mateo he'd turned him into a puddle.

"Bet you're fucking this mouth every morning, aren't you?" Jeff finally said.

"You got that right. First thing."

"Ever watched his lips slide along another man's cock like this?"

"No, sir."

"You liking it?"

"Gonna shoot if I touch myself, sir. Does that answer the question?"

Because it's your cock his lips are sliding along, he wanted to say. Why did that feel like too much given all the other lines they'd crossed?

"Get those pants off him, *papi,*" Mateo ordered.

Still sucking, Buckley pushed Jeff's dress pants down past his hips, then his knees. Finally, he had to slide off Jeff's cock so he could pull the man's puddled pants out from his ankles.

"Shirt too," Mateo ordered.

Buckley complied. He half expected the two men to start kissing passionately given how close their mouths were again. When they didn't, Mateo realized he'd managed to place his boyfriend entirely under his command. Once Jeff's dress shirt was off, Buckley looked to Mateo with wide-eyed eagerness, and with a thrill, Mateo realized his boyfriend was asking for his next move.

"Do you want to touch him?"

Buckley nodded. "Yes."

"Where?"

"His chest. I want to feel his chest."

"Okay, you can touch his chest. But you have to kiss him while you do it so he knows how grateful you are for his cock."

Not touching himself was sweet torture. Even though they'd never been in the same room before tonight, the two men he loved desperately were both naked and under his control. For the first time, he was dominating Jeff, and he was doing it in a way that felt right for them both—for all three of them—by offering up his boyfriend, who hungered for submission, and who'd unwittingly set the stage for their forbidden desires to bloom.

"Buckley, back up."

Startled, Buckley complied, swallowing, turning to face Mateo as if he'd done something wrong. "Take your clothes off. Show the master sergeant what a sexy body you have." There it was, the faint flicker of hesitation, the insecurity about always having been what he called a *thick boy*. But Mateo knew the best treatment for this insanity was to aggressively and forcefully remind him what a sexy fucking bitch he was at every turn.

Buckley unbuttoned his pants. Jeff started toward him to help.

"Stay right there," Mateo said.

Jeff, unaccustomed to being bossed around by junior Marines present or former—froze in place. When he saw Mateo wasn't kidding, he sucked in a deep breath through his nose, then returned his lascivious attention to his intended target. The slow hesitancy with which Buckley undressed was a stark counterpart to the confidence and speed with which he'd devoured Jeff's cock. Another reminder that he too often put others' needs ahead of his own, something Mateo had become determined to rid him of one explosive fuck at a time.

He slid out of one pant leg, then the other before kicking them aside. When he pushed his briefs down over his hips, his cock popped up and slapped his navel, as hard as it would get when Mateo was deep inside him and driving down on his special spot.

"Turn all the way around so the master sergeant can see how beautiful you are."

His eyes fluttering closed, swallowing carefully, Buckley did as instructed. Mateo caught Jeff gently stroking his own cock.

"Hands at your sides, Master Sergeant."

This time Jeff laughed softly under his breath, as if Mateo's show of dominance was an adorable little game. He obeyed, however, and by the time Buckley had completed his slow turn, the older man's eyes were lust glazed.

But Mateo was more concerned with Buckley's comfort level. It had exploded out of the box, this fantasy, while everything else they'd done together had been carefully scripted, sometimes even rehearsed. Was there a way to set ground rules on the fly?

"*Papi*," Mateo asked softly. "Is the dry cleaning back?"

This was their soft and secret code, a polite way for Mateo to inquire if Buckley was prepared to get fully and aggressively fucked without forcing him to go into specifics that might kill the mood.

Buckley shook his head.

If Jeff was curious about this exchange, he kept it to himself. "You're such a good boy, *papi*. Look how hard the master sergeant is for you." Buckley's eyes fluttered in that special way they did when he was about to come, and suddenly Mateo was thinking of a term he'd only heard a few times in life, and mostly while researching sex stuff on the internet. *Praise kink.*

His boyfriend had a praise kink, and he could see it in the effect the words *good boy* had on him—flushing his milky skin, making his cock jump and his already hungry breaths intensify. Something about their role-play—as one sided as it had been—had fed this kink of Buckley's for a year now. Fed both his kinks, Mateo realized. By pretending to be stock characters Mateo fantasized about, he'd fulfilled his own fantasy of watching Mateo with other men. And by turning himself into Mateo's fantasy each time, he'd solicited the praise and validation he was after. But both seemed like longer back routes to a place Mateo could take him to more directly.

With Jeff's help.

"He really is a good boy, isn't he, Master Sergeant? He's got a smart mouth, but deep down all he wants to do is please."

Jeff nodded, eyebrow raised. He reached for his own cock again, and Mateo snapped his fingers.

"You forgive him, right? He's a good boy who wants to make it up to you. Take him to bed. Let my boyfriend show you what a good, hungry slut he is."

Jeff slid an arm around Buckley's shoulders, guiding him through the sliding double doors that opened on to the bedroom. Mateo rose and followed. He liked the fact that he was still wearing his unbuttoned dress shirt while the men before him were totally naked, like the rumpled Ralph Lauren was some kind of master of debauched ceremonies costume.

As he and Buckley sank onto the comforter together, Jeff transformed his lascivious attention into pure, tender affection, hugging and caressing and kissing and stroking Buckley at a leisurely, lingering pace. Buckley, for his part, looked like he was melting into the bigger man's kisses, losing himself in his powerful embrace.

"He worked so hard to get you here tonight," Mateo said softly. "He wanted so bad to make me happy. He wants to make you happy too, Master Sergeant."

Mouths locked, Jeff had taken one of Buckley's nipples in one hand and was tweaking it hard and furiously. Buckley's mouth popped open against Jeff's. That and the strangled cry of pleasure in his throat must have let Jeff know he'd hit a sensitive target.

"There you go," Mateo said. "You found one of his spots. I'll tell you where the others are too. That way you can really show him what a good boy he is."

"Babe," Buckley gasped. "Get down here with us. Please."

"I second that," Jeff growled before devouring Buckley's lips with another kiss.

"Can't. Gonna blow the second one of you touches me. And I want to enjoy every minute of my birthday present." Bending down slightly, Mateo put a hand on Buckley's hip and rolled him gently onto his back. "I can help though."

He spread Buckley's thighs, then traced one finger down the inside of each one, making his boyfriend shiver twice in quick succession, showing Jeff a new set of paths to driving Buckley wild. Two of them, a matching set. Jeff took the trip with his caressing hands, as Buckley gritted his teeth to keep from crying out. Clearly hungry for more of the same reaction, Jeff slid down Buckley's body, replacing his caressing hands and tracing fingers with his tongue. A tongue that worked its way up to the underside of Buckley's balls before swallowing him in one forceful move.

The sight of his muscled former crew chief inhaling his boyfriend's cock drove Mateo even closer to the edge. His eyes had fluttered shut so the warm wetness on one hand caught him by surprise. Buckley was sucking Mateo's fingers with the same eagerness Jeff was using on his cock. The remote kissing thing had been tingly and magical, but this was a white-hot shock that went through his whole body, like an electric current was traveling through all three men at the same time.

Puppy-dog eager, Buckley's blue eyes gazed up at him.

Jeff was caressing the underside of Buckley's balls while sucking his cock, then his fingers started to play a gentle tune across Buckley's hole. Apparently he'd interpreted their code correctly because he wasn't using half the force of which he was capable.

"Baby," Buckley whispered into Mateo's fingers.

"What do you need my sweet, beautiful boy?"

Buckley hesitated, which left Mateo wondering what sort of request could be wilder than all the things they were already doing.

"Show him how much you missed him," Buckley finally whispered. "Please. Show Jeff how much you missed him."

Jeff stopped sucking but he didn't stop stroking, even as he looked up at Mateo with a hard glint in his eyes and spit-slick lips. Truth was, that look he always talked about Jeff having, the one that could make a guy drop their undies in ten seconds flat, had worked a few wonders on him as well.

"How do you want me to do that, *papi*?" Mateo asked, feeling his dominance slipping away. The look in Jeff's eyes, the need in Buckley's voice—these two men owned him now and probably forever.

"Just give him a kiss. That's all."

Jeff rose to his knees on the other side of Buckley's prone body. Mateo beheld the sight of him. Brawny and masculine. A different kind of beauty from Buckley's, for sure. All hard angles to Buckley's luscious brawn. It had hurt and angered him to discover that he couldn't bend himself to the full arc of Jeff's desire for him. But he'd bent plenty. He'd slept inside the man's powerful embrace like a baby that last night in San Diego, and a part of him had longed for it ever since. And then those kisses. Those kisses he'd thought about ever since that wild weekend. Kisses that had been enough to make him spill in Jeff's stroking hand.

They were face-to-face again, and this room was nicer and more beautiful, and the beautiful man between them wasn't some rando who'd skitter out the door as soon as this was done. There'd be no hurrying out the door as soon as this was done. For any of them. He'd make sure of that.

"I missed you, Cano."

"If you missed me that bad, use my first name for a change."

Jeff cocked one eyebrow. "You've been calling me master

sergeant all night."

"Kiss me, Jeff."

The man's powerful hand wrapped around the back of Mateo's head. Mateo felt his lips part in surrender, and then, at last, they were tasting each other again. The roughness of the man's cheeks and chin a delicious counterpoint to the slick, smooth kisses he and Buckley had shared for a year now.

Beneath them, Buckley erupted with a desperate cry, creamy threads firing across his stomach. The sounds ripping from him were as frenzied as the ones he'd released in the kitchen the night before. Like the pleasure was so overwhelming Buckley had to fight it with gritted teeth as his body bucked and heaved or else it would blow him apart.

"Fuck," Jeff whispered, staring down at the man beneath him in what looked like wonder. "Goddamn."

Mateo reached around and grabbed the back of Jeff's head, then he brought their foreheads together as he furiously stroked his own cock. "Paint him. Paint our boy."

Our boy? Had he really called Buckley *their* boy?

If it was a mistake, he'd regret it later. For now, there was only the train of release barreling toward his cock.

Mateo went first, and when the yell tore from him, Jeff started laughing with delight, and then suddenly Mateo was struggling to stay upright on his knees as he jerked and spasmed. Jeff followed a second later. He'd forgotten the majestic way the man came. Buckley climaxed like a writhing wild thing. When Mateo shot, he always felt like he was about to pass out. The acme of Jeff Braxton's bliss made the man look focused and determined, teeth gritted, body rigid and stilled as he stroked himself with steady, experienced force, aiming his cock like a weapon.

Buckley had scooted down the bed, looking both dazed and delighted as he gently spread their slick loads across his bare chest, dressing his nipples with it. Eyes fluttering closed as if its feel made his skin tingle.

The next thing he knew, he'd wilted to the mattress beside Buckley. Jeff had done the same on the other side.

As their breaths deepened, he worried that reality and guilt—his old nemesis—might crowd in. But before it could, Buckley said, "If either of you fall asleep before you clean me up, I'm putting your underwear in the freezer."

8

If he was going to jet, now was the time, Jeff thought.

Mateo had gone to run the bath. Buckley was half conscious next to him. He could scoot out before the other man came back. Even if Buckley threw himself across the door, he wouldn't be outnumbered.

But when the man sighed and snuggled up into him before he could put the plan into action, his warmth filled Jeff like the first cool drink after a grueling trek through scorched desert. He returned the embrace before he could think twice about it.

When was the last time sex had left him this spent, this utterly content? He couldn't remember.

He'd had his fair share of wild experiences, guest starred for plenty of couples in his day. Hell, he'd even taken a chance on a Grindr hookup who wouldn't share a face pic only to have the door to a La Jolla hotel room opened by an A-list celebrity he'd lusted after since seeing him in his first superhero flick. Apparently the guy had been in town for Comic-Con.

For the most part, those experiences had been hotter in the retelling than in the execution, the stuff he'd brag about with some of his buddies. The couples awkwardly scooted him out the door once the deed was done, and the celebrity had smelled of too much liquid courage.

This had been something else entirely. This had been…Mateo.

And Buckley. Who somehow knew me down to my core without ever meeting me.

It felt like loving the same man had made them instantly intimate with each other. In ways that went beyond the physical.

Our boy.

Mateo's words thrummed in his head. They'd pushed him over the edge, causing him to erupt. The idea that he and Mateo could have someone to share, someone wild and fierce and eager to surrender to them both.

He tried to remember the last time he'd lost control like this. With Mateo, of course. In San Diego. For over a year and half now, he'd assumed that trip had ruined everything. But if it had set the stage for this, maybe that wasn't true. But what was *this?* What had they started?

And was it true he'd lost control? He'd spent the night chipping away at Buckley's agenda and eventually he'd revealed it.

"Alright, gents," Mateo said from the bathroom door. "Let's get clean."

Jeff rolled to one side. Mateo had lost the shirt. The sight of him naked and leaning against the doorframe with his arms crossed over his smooth brown chest made Jeff's head spin. He smiled, extended one hand, and helped Jeff to his feet. As soon as they were face-to-face, their mouths met. This time they kissed without a mad race to orgasm driving them.

The next thing he knew, the two of them were guiding Buckley into the dimly lit bathroom where sweeps of honey-colored marble flickered in the light of the candles Mateo had relocated from the villa's sitting room. The massive jacuzzi tub was almost full. Buckley stumbled for a few steps, clearly still spent in more ways than one, before Mateo guided all of them into warm water, positioning Buckley in the middle.

As their soapy hands kneaded and caressed the man between them, Buckley's soft cooing sounds turned to long, throaty groans. His pleasure was infectious, and Jeff felt a stirring in his balls. No small feat for a guy in his forties who'd just come so hard he thought his eyes might pop out.

"Damn, *papi*," Mateo cooed, and that's when Jeff saw that Buckley was going hard again in the bathwater.

"I like being your boy," Buckley whispered.

They were quiet words, casual words. Gentle, even. But they seemed full of promise and potential, and in the watery silence that followed, they hung in the steam over the tub as both men continued working their soapy hands across Buckley's neck and shoulders, then up into his armpits.

Did he mean Mateo's boy? Or did he mean he belonged to both of them?

Eventually, these vague and slippery possessive pronouns would have to grow more defined. But for now there was only the gentle sounds and sights of a man being gently undone by the work of four powerful hands.

Buckley leaned back. Jeff worked his hands up the center of his chest. Mateo focused on Buckley's outstretched arm, a wicked smile on his face at the sight of the tenderness between the two men in front of him.

"Normally a bottom has to get railed to get this kind of treatment," Buckley said.

"Yeah, well, it sounded like it wasn't the right moment." Jeff kissed the side of Buckley's neck.

"Stay the night," Buckley said quietly, clearly struggling to focus through the pleasure both men were giving him. "He should stay the night, right, babe?"

Mateo nodded with an eager smile.

"Not sure that's a good idea," Jeff said before he could stop himself.

Mateo's smile faded. Slowly, Buckley turned over in the water until he was eye-to-eye with Jeff.

"Do you ever let go long enough to let anyone take care of you, Master Sergeant?"

The words lanced through him.

They should have hurt, but the man who'd spoken them hadn't said them in anger. He'd said them in need.

And that's what he felt coming from both of the men sharing the tub with him—need. Lust had been fed by their wild three-way, distance bridged by his arrival earlier that night. Basic cravings had been satisfied. If they still wanted him to stay, they were being driven by something else. They didn't want a guest star or a sex toy. They wanted *him*, and it had been a very long time since a sexual experience of any kind had left him feeling that way. People wanted Jeff Braxton's Marine Corps experience, they wanted him to command, to train, and occasionally, they wanted him to fuck them into the wall while calling them dirty names. But they never wanted him to be messy and hungry and needy in expensive hotel sheets for hours on end.

"You're pretty frank now that we've gotten sweaty together."

"As if. You didn't nickname me firecracker after two minutes because I mince words."

Jeff's eyes met Mateo's. "Is this how he charmed you off your feet?"

Mateo shrugged. "A little. But I didn't need the hard sell like you did. He had me from day one. Besides, you've got a helluva of a mouth on you too, Master Sergeant."

Buckley sat up. Then, smiling, he sank back against his beautiful boyfriend. For a second, Jeff thought he was being punished with a bit of distance. Then he realized it was the opposite. Buckley was setting the table with a two-course breakfast that would be waiting for him in the morning if he decided to spend the night.

He felt a lecture brewing.

They should keep this fun, that's all. And maybe fun meant once or twice a month and no more. Then they wouldn't lose their heads. But the lecture didn't come. Instead, he found himself drinking in the sight of their beautiful young bodies tangled together in warm water turned sudsy. Light flickering off their wet smooth skin. What a pair they made. Mateo, tall, bronze, and solid, his gaze steady and piercing as Jeff's, his long, muscled arms wrapped around Buckley's thick, compact, creamy white body that always seemed coiled and ready to spring into pleasure giving. A promise buttressed by the constantly mischievous glint in his big blue searching eyes.

"Watcha thinking, Master Sergeant?" Mateo finally asked.

I'm thinking you're two sirens and I'm a helpless sailor you're about to drag off to a pleasure island. But what he said was, "I'm thinking we should ditch rank if we're gonna keep doing this."

"The master sergeant thing's hot, though," Buckley said softly. "I mean, I don't even know what they do, but still...hot. Besides, Mateo's not a Marine anymore."

Jeff reached under the water and squeezed one of Buckley's feet, bringing it close to the surface while kneading it in a way that made the man's eyes hood and his lips pout with suddenly deep breaths. "Got yourself a chaser here, Cano."

"What's that?" Buckley asked.

Mateo shook his head. "Old-school term for a gay guy with a

Marine fetish."

"Excuse me," Buckley said. "I will not be lumped in with some creeper who cruises Oceanside trying to blow enlisted guys in his car."

"Hey," Jeff said, "don't judge. A lot of those so-called creepers were sexy as hell. I should know. I hooked up with plenty of 'em."

"See, Master Sergeant?" Mateo asked. "This isn't the craziest thing you've ever done."

"So is this a DP I'm being invited to in the morning?"

Buckley furrowed his brow as if considering it deeply, but Jeff figured it was the killer foot massage he was giving him that had reduced him to silence. Mateo laughed and patted Buckley's chest. "I think we're going to need to work up to that one. My boy's talented, but that's Olympic level. Right?" He kissed Buckley on the nape of his neck.

"We'll work up to it," Buckley answered, staring into Jeff's eyes.

Working up to something took time. It was, dare he say, a commitment.

"And I should glove up if we go that route, know what I mean? Unless this isn't your first time hosting a visitor."

It was a simple request that raised complicated questions. He took a pill every day to prevent HIV and got tested for pretty much everything else on the regular. In light of both things, his condom use hadn't been anywhere near as regular as it had been back when he'd first come out. But if Mateo and Buckley had been monogamous up until last night, they probably weren't on PrEP. Had they, though? Suddenly he cared whether or not they had. Suddenly he hoped desperately to be the first third they'd played with.

Maybe even the last third they ever played with.

Are you playing, Braxton? Or did you make a giant fucking mistake here?

"We're not on PrEP, if that's what you're asking," Buckley finally said. "You're the first."

Like he could see right through him, this guy.

"I'll stay," he finally said.

Visible relief overtook both men.

Slowly, Buckley crawled forward through the water, studying Jeff carefully, as if their closeness would have more impact now that he'd agreed to spend the night. When their mouths met again, he feared the kiss wouldn't have the same flushing heat to it. Perhaps their initial sparks had been thrown off by the fire of the forbidden. But as Buckley's mouth melted under his, Jeff's spine felt incandescent. Mateo's face was inches away suddenly, and then it was his lips Jeff was tasting. The water started to go lukewarm around them. He lost sight of which man he was kissing, which man was groping or caressing him. Because he didn't care.

And he thought, *Heaven. I have found heaven. And I did it by walking straight into my fears.*

After toweling himself off, Mateo headed for bed, but Buckley paused in the doorway, turning to face Jeff, who was still drying himself.

"I'll get the lights," Buckley whispered. Jeff wasn't sure what the guy meant, which must have been clear in his expression because Buckley added, "They've got dimmers, and he doesn't do well with those. I took them all out at our place. When they fade they remind him of when the Osprey pitched forward and—"

"Gotcha." Jeff felt foolish for not having put it together and a little childish for thinking Buckley's furtive whispers were a prelude to more shenanigans.

As he slipped into bed next to him, Jeff wondered if Mateo had ever been surfing again after his near drowning, but the last thing he wanted to do was ask. He wondered if, when it came to the accident, Mateo could bring himself to say aloud those four letters that bedeviled so many military men and women—PTSD. And his ignorance on these matters made him feel a twinge of guilt. A twinge that might have felt more like a sword in the gut if he hadn't been holding Mateo in both arms.

The ache and longing he'd felt over the past year and a half whenever he thought of the man's beautiful brown eyes or gentle laugh had been removed from him in the course of one wild night. And by a man who ignited a new appetite in him that felt just as powerful.

Once he'd finished turning off all the lights one by one, Buckley slipped into bed on the other side of Mateo, and in a few seconds they'd made a snuggly sandwich out of the birthday boy.

9

Jeff's sleep was deep and dreamless. Combat memories often spiked in the minutes right before waking. Not this morning, not with these men.

When he woke, Mateo's head was resting on his chest.

A gentle rush of water came from the bathroom.

Buckley had left them alone together.

"If memory serves…" Mateo whispered, then he gently sucked on Jeff's right nipple, sending arcs of pleasure across his chest, down his sides, before they found their way to his balls. He moved to the left one, then after a while of sweet torture, his lips found Jeff's and he whispered, "You're such a man," as if this was a wondrous fact he'd just arrived at recently.

But Jeff thought he knew what he meant. Or at least he hoped he did.

He was running his hands over Jeff's hair-dusted chest, then his arms, as if his presence there was a miracle. His caresses were studded by the occasional well-timed pinch and tweak. Buckley was fiery, boyish bottom energy. Jeff was something harder and older, and so Mateo, who was grinding his hardening cock against Jeff's thigh as he rubbed the expanse of the older man's body, was letting him know how much he hungered for both.

"The man who saved my life," Mateo whispered as he gently gripped the base of Jeff's cock, which was rock hard and ready.

"A world without you in it is not a world I want to live in."

It was like the words had been forced from him by a higher

power. He'd whispered some variation of them into his pillow a thousand times, but always alone. And the words had felt hypocritical given how he'd cut the guy loose. But in the dark of his own apartment, into that foggy space between sleep and waking where dreams seemed real and fantasies possible, he'd whispered the truth that had brought him to this moment.

Mateo's breath left him in a startled huff.

Jeff had finally confessed to the reckless love that had driven him to nearly sacrifice his own life to save Mateo from what had looked like certain death. And he'd done it while caressing the side of Mateo's face.

Slowly, Mateo took one of his fingertips between his lips and sucked—hungrily, submissively, worshipfully—before returning his attention to Jeff's cock.

"Is this allowed?" Jeff asked.

Gazing up at him confidently, Mateo answered with a long, slow lick up the length of Jeff's shaft. Then he swallowed the man with more skill than he'd demonstrated that night in San Diego. Another sign of Buckley's training and guidance. The sweet, shy Marine Jeff had once taken under his wing had been transformed into a sexual powerhouse, and he was rocking the foundations of Jeff's world.

He wasn't doing it alone, however.

The bathroom door slid sideways and Buckley emerged, naked, his white skin gone pink in places from the shower, a heady combo of freshly scrubbed innocence and raw lust. Any doubts that he and Mateo might have gotten ahead of themselves were dispelled when Buckley started stroking his cock at the sight of both men tangled together in bed.

"Sorry, baby," Mateo said, still stroking. "I couldn't resist."

"Don't want you to." Buckley smiled. "Fun bag?"

Mateo let the slick head of Jeff's cock pop from his lips and pointed behind him. "Top drawer."

At the dresser beneath the flat-screen TV, Buckley followed Mateo's instruction and pulled out a toiletry bag, then went stone still at the sight of whatever was inside. Focusing on anything other than the pleasure Mateo was giving him was a challenge, but Jeff couldn't ignore that Buckley's upper back was shaking with silent laughter. He pulled something from the bag and turned around, revealing a massive veiny dildo. "Um, babe?"

Still stroking Jeff's cock, Mateo looked back over one shoulder and laughed. "Surprise. I figured it'd be hard to get my hands on a zucchini." Mateo smiled down at Jeff's cock in his stroking hand. "No idea we'd end up with the real thing."

And with that, Mateo swallowed Jeff's cock again.

As Mateo sucked, Buckley sank down into the chair in the corner, reached into the open fun bag nearby for a bottle of lube. The intent expression on his face sent chills up Jeff's spine. When he bent both knees and rested the soles of his feet on the edge of the chair's seat, Jeff realized what he was about to do; his breath caught and his balls tensed up in the same dizzying instant. The sight of a confident bottom working himself over with a big thick toy had always done him in. But this was Buckley, his firecracker. The man who'd brought Mateo back to him, the one who'd given him something entirely new and unexpected in return.

It was sweet torture, giving himself over to the pleasure Mateo's mouth was giving while watching Buckley carefully lube himself up. Jeff tried to memorize every confident circling of Buckley's three fingers, and then, the careful and skillful way he slowly speared himself on the sex toy that was Jeff but not Jeff.

He could only keep his eyes open a few seconds at a time or else he was going to erupt too soon.

Mateo, his beautiful, sweet Mateo, devouring his cock with newly acquired skill.

Buckley, vulnerable and open and unashamed as he filled himself with the special present his boyfriend had brought as a surprise.

A present that was supposed to bring Jeff's presence into the room. Into their bed.

Buckley fought to keep his eyes open amidst the blend of pleasure and resistance. Clearly, he didn't want to miss a beat of the work Mateo was performing on Jeff's pleasure-paralyzed body.

Mateo stopped his sucking and looked back over one shoulder.

"You like watching us, *papi?*"

Buckley nodded slowly, fucking himself long and slow. "No stopping," he managed through his heavy breaths.

"What else do you want to see?" Mateo asked.

Eyes closed, stuttering out a breath, he smiled. But Jeff thought it was pretty clear he'd dragged that thick girth and those plastic veins over his G-spot harder than he'd meant to, and he was fighting an eruption. There was, in Jeff's opinion, no more beautiful sight than the pleasure that overtook a bottom when you ground into them in just the right place.

"If Jeff's the reason you eat ass like a champ, I want to see him prove it."

Mateo laughed and sank back onto his haunches.

His heart had been racing before. Now it thundered.

He'd never tasted Mateo before. Guided and directed him on the ass of that stripper, sure. But he'd never been down there himself, no matter how many times he'd dreamed of it, so when Mateo turned around to face his boyfriend, then slowly bent forward onto his elbows, offering up those smooth, brown globes with their fine dusting of jet-black hair along the crack, Jeff had to be careful as he rose to his knees. If his cock brushed the bedding, he might empty himself onto the comforter.

He bent forward, caressed Mateo's ass cheeks for the first time, feeling like he might cry with joy. It was time for the rim parade, a trick he'd taught Mateo a year and a half ago. Three different types of licks in succession to see which one gets the best response. Long and wide and up the center of his crack, followed by a mad flicker around the edge of his hole, finished off with a couple deep, punching tongue fucks. Most guys were a fan of at least one.

Long and slow had Mateo groaning into the comforter. So did another, and another. When he raised his head from the majestic heaven of the man's cheeks, he saw Buckley spearing himself hard and fast. "See?" he said, eyes glassy and wild. "There are other ways you can top my boyfriend, Master Sergeant."

Jeff went back in, unleashing a series of mad flickers that made Mateo whimper and cry. The sweetest sound Jeff had ever heard. The deep, punching tongue fuck was greeted with silence, probably 'cause Mateo was truly a top. That was fine. He had two techniques to work with, and he attacked them with vigor. He'd never heard Mateo make noises like this, not even when he was tasting a fine dessert. The aggressiveness with which Buckley was fucking himself, and the dazzled, wondrous expression on his face as he did so, suggested he hadn't heard his boyfriend make noises like this either.

No more rank or nicknames, his name moaned in a pleading tone by the man who drove him wild.

His hand found Mateo's cock. Rock hard, leaking sap. Jeff licked and flickered, kissed and nibbled. Years of hunger unleashed in a way he'd never dreamed possible.

He had to stop or he was going to come, and his appetite had spread beyond the beautiful man sprawled ass up and face down in front of him.

Buckley's eyes widened when he saw Jeff was on his knees again, but he was slowly grinding the dildo in and out of his hole, his nostrils flaring and his own cock a throbbing pink rod against his milk-pale stomach.

Suddenly they were both approaching Buckley like stalking lions.

Jeff sank to his knees. Mateo did the same next to him. Buckley let out a soft, startled cry when Jeff took the end of the dildo from his grip and began to replicate the motions Buckley had been using to drive himself to the brink. His eyes turned wide and expectant, his breaths whistling through his moist, parted lips.

"Well, well. Look at what we have here," Jeff said. "Damn, you're right, Cano. Your boyfriend's one hungry slut."

"Yeah, and apparently he's been keeping it a secret just how hungry he is."

"Looks like the secret's out." Jeff released the dildo's end, and Mateo took over. Buckley let out a stuttering breath at having command of his pleasure transferred from one man to the other. He reached for his cock. Jeff batted it away. "Oh, no you don't, firecracker. You want to play games, tell lies, get us all hot and bothered and out of our minds, then we get to play with this ass as much as we want. When we're done, you're done, and not a second before."

"That's right, Master Sergeant. This ass is ours."

It sounded like Buckley was trying to speak, but his words became incomprehensible. Mateo slowly speared him all the way to the hilt. Buckley's slitted eyes turned white as he pressed the crown of his head back into the chair's cushion.

Ours again. Jeff's cock jerked at the simple, short word.

The title.

The brand.

"Can't believe he's been keeping this a secret," Mateo said, "how much he wanted the two of us together. How hard he'd get watching you eat my ass."

Mateo released the dildo. Jeff took that as his cue to take control again.

"Makes me wonder what other secrets he's been keeping," Mateo said softly. He'd gently seized both of Buckley's nipples in his fingers and was playing some music on them that made Buckley whimper and give his boyfriend a look that appeared desperate with hunger.

"I don't think any of us are gonna have a secret left by the time we leave this room," Jeff said.

"Me too." Mateo bent forward, gave his boyfriend a gentle kiss on the lips, but Buckley was gasping so desperately from the forceful sex toy fuck Jeff was giving him he could barely return it. "But I can tell you one of his."

"Oh yeah?" Jeff asked.

Mateo nodded, then he sank down to all fours on the carpet, bringing himself eye level with the thick pink dildo sliding in and out of his boyfriend's hole. He caressed one of Buckley's slick, pink cheeks gently. "This right here," he said softly, then he gave his ass cheek a kiss, barely inches from where Jeff was spearing. "This isn't just an ass, Master Sergeant. It's a pussy. And pretty soon you're going to fill it with your cock."

When Buckley yowled, Jeff thought maybe he was angry his boyfriend had given away his special nickname for his ass. Then he saw strands of pearly white cream lacing Buckley's sweaty stomach. Jeff switched to long, slow, deep, piercing strokes, determined to drive every last drop of seed from the man as he spasmed and jerked and tried to catch his breath with a series of grunts, groans, and growls that made him sound both furious and joyful at once.

Mateo's joy was undeniable. He cackled and rose to his knees, clearly delighted to have sent his boyfriend over the edge with the use of a single dirty word. Furiously, he stroked his cock over his boyfriend's stomach.

The sight roused Buckley from his stupor. He reached forward and tapped Mateo on the ass a few times. Recognizing some unspoken signal, Mateo scooted forward, rising up off his knees, holding himself up with one hand braced against the chair's arm. Suddenly his erupting cock was between Buckley's lips, and the guy was drinking his boyfriend's seed like it was chocolate milk. Inhaling the stuff with an intimacy and confidence that made Jeff blow.

By the time he was done, Mateo had fallen to the carpet next to the floor so he could watch the final moments of the show, and when

Jeff blinked and caught his breath, he saw Buckley spreading the tendrils of Jeff's creamy load up across his stomach and in a lazy circle around his navel. But his blue eyes were locked on Jeff's face, and his drowsy half smile seemed to say, *You're next.*

Jeff kissed him.

It should have been nothing considering all they'd done to each other, but there was something about the force of it, the spontaneity of it, that captured all three of them in a silent grip. It was a kiss that said *I see you and want you to be mine.* And Buckley returned it with drowsy, spent hunger. And when he pulled back slowly, Jeff looked to Mateo as if he'd been caught doing something bad, which also seemed absurd. But Mateo was smiling, eyes hooded, chewing his bottom lip. A relaxed but calculating look. Like he'd seen something deeper and more complicated in this split-second kiss—and he liked it.

He'd fallen for Mateo long ago.

Was he falling for Buckley now too?

Could Mateo see it?

Could Buckley?

"Bottoms get first shower." Buckley slid to the floor. He waddled to the bathroom door. The dildo still speared him to the hilt. He gave his ass a little shake, then slid the bathroom door shut behind him.

"Wild child," Jeff said.

"I like firecracker," Mateo said. "Firecracker's perfect."

It felt like another subtle commitment, Mateo allowing Jeff to give his boyfriend a new, enduring nickname.

A few seconds later, as they listened to the shower spray from the bathroom, Mateo snuggled up against him. Sitting naked on the carpeted floor wasn't the most comfortable position, but they were both too exhausted to move. And Mateo was gently caressing Jeff's chest, then his stomach, and even though the carpet was a little rough under his bare ass, Jeff thought, *I could stay here forever, which probably means it's time to go.*

When Buckley emerged, Mateo told Jeff to hit the shower ahead of him.

Figuring the two boyfriends probably wanted to talk over recent events with him out of earshot, Jeff headed into the shower, a cold, prickly feeling spreading across his skin. Alone, under the spray, taking too long to soap his hair as his thoughts spiraled outward, he tried not to give himself over to dark imaginings about what they were saying in the other room.

Maybe they were plotting how to gracefully get rid of him. It would make sense. If one of them was going to freak out and regret the past few hours, now would be the perfect time.

Hell, maybe he'd thrown too much cold water on everything with his condom request the night before. Introduced too much reality into the crazed fantasy they'd lived out for several hours. Should he have just taken Buckley raw if the guy had wanted him to, medical realities be damned? He was tested on the regular and was confident the risk of giving Buckley anything was lower than low. Now, he wished he had. The thought that he might never get a taste of Mateo and Buckley again after this morning filled him with panic.

He hated feeling this way.

Vulnerable. A word that made his skin crawl.

That's what walking into the party last night had made him feel. It's how he felt when he decided to stay at the party after Buckley's deception had been revealed. And it's how he felt now.

It's how it felt to want something, want someone.

In this case, *two* someones.

But walking through those vulnerable moments had given him a night that had rocked his world, taken him to new heights of pleasure. So maybe if he could stick this out, keep his cool, not rush for the exits until they gestured to them politely, he'd be greeted with another fantasy made reality.

Problem was, he didn't have a change of clothes.

And maybe that was a sign.

It really was time for him to head out. If the men in the other room were trying to figure out how to say it, maybe they'd follow up their words with an invite for round two. That would be good. Beyond good. Every time he thought of the moment he and Mateo had stalked across the floor toward Buckley's chair, two hungry beasts working in tandem, the hotness of it—the *rightness* of it—quickened his breaths and tightened his balls.

Our boy. He could be our boy.

His head was spinning by the time he stepped from the shower.

He'd tried to talk himself back to reality and ended up somewhere between hope and despair. He was seven years old again and his uncle was accusing him of destroying another relationship, another home, because he'd been too wild, too free.

So by the time he opened the door to the bedroom, he was beginning to phrase the words of his graceful exit speech. That's when he saw a neatly folded outfit sitting atop the freshly smoothed-down comforter. A pair of jeans and a navy-blue polo shirt. Mateo's, probably, but about his size. The two men were standing on the other side of the bed, speaking in hushed whispers. Buckley was dressed in khaki shorts and a V-neck tee. Mateo was still deliciously naked, which made their casual embrace feel somehow naughty.

"You can wear that to lunch," Mateo said.

Jeff nodded, studying the clothes. "Lunch."

"After that," Buckley said, "it's no big deal since we'll come back here and we won't have to wear any clothes at all."

Jeff huffed with laughter, hoping his relief hadn't turned him red.

Mateo was facing him now, looking serious. The scene before him was the reverse of what he'd dreaded in the shower. They didn't want him to go. They wanted him to stay. But for how long?

"Here's the deal," Mateo said. "We've got a late checkout tomorrow. We want you to stay until then. And until then, we just…go with this. Enjoy it. Then around four tomorrow afternoon we can sit down and have a big talk, and you can pick this apart and tell us how it was a bad idea and we should never do it again."

"You really think I'd say that?"

"Yes," Mateo said. "Because I know you. And you have every right to say it."

"But we're not promising to agree with you," Buckley added.

His laughter got the best of him. And there was no hiding the relief in it. Then both men were moving toward him, and the next thing Jeff knew Buckley was sliding a blue polo over his head and Mateo was dragging a pair of his own white briefs up his legs.

How, after all the debauched things they'd done together, could this be the sexiest thing that had ever happened to him? Two men he was crazy about dressing him with gentle but determined hands, encouraging him not to run.

10

Sapphire Cove's sundrenched main restaurant sat between the bustling lobby and a soaring wall of plate glass that offered an expansive view of coastal mountains plunging toward the sparkling Pacific.

Buckley was giddy over the fact that he'd gotten both men to agree to his four p.m. Sunday rule. Now, he figured, they could all stretch their limbs and enjoy every inch of space inside this wild weekend they'd declared for themselves. Tomorrow, they could worry about the consequences. Tomorrow, they could talk about what this all meant, and, more importantly, what it might turn into.

Once the server had taken their orders, Buckley said, "Truth or dare?"

Jeff laughed.

Mateo glanced around at the packed tables nearby. "I'm thinking the dare part might be kinda adventurous, *papi*. Even for us."

"We do the truth part here, and we bank all the dares. If someone takes that option."

"Bank them?" Jeff asked with a wry smile.

"For later. In the room." Buckley waggled his eyebrows.

Until tomorrow's deadline arrived, he thought it best to schedule their activities, keep them engaged with the steamier side of their adventure in throupling. He didn't want to overdo it. Didn't want to turn into chirpy, needy, ten-year-old Buckley, trying to hold his parents' focus before their minds wandered to their next luxury vacation—without him. But too much idle time might lead to insecurity and doubt. Better they make the most of the hours they had left together before *real talk* entered the chat.

"I'm down," Jeff said, "if you go first. Cano?"

Mateo nodded and said, "And Jeff gets first question."

Buckley nodded. "Deal."

"Truth or dare?" Jeff asked.

"Truth," Buckley answered.

Jeff sipped his mimosa, studying Buckley. His intent looks carried more power now, and Buckley found himself suddenly flushed and breathless under its force.

"What's your biggest fear?" Jeff asked.

"Well, when I was a kid, it was being kidnapped."

"And now?"

Buckley thought about it for a moment, then told himself that spending a lot of time on this kind of answer was usually a sign you were making one up. "Getting lost. Like on a hike. You know, getting turned around and losing my way and being too far from civilization to call. I'm not a big wilderness person, so..."

"You need people," Jeff said. "I mean, that's what both of those are about, right? Getting lost, being kidnapped when you're young. Those are both about being alone. Being abandoned."

He felt himself flush. "I guess."

"It's nothing to be ashamed of."

Buckley cut his eyes to Jeff's, startled to be read in this way. For some reason, the admission, that he'd spent most of his younger years feeling like his parents might lose track of him, *did* make him feel ashamed. Like the feelings were his fault, the cause irrelevant.

"I don't know..." Buckley's confidence left him. Jeff Braxton seemed to have that effect. "Do I really have any right to complain? I mean, yeah, so my parents were...eccentric."

"If by eccentric you mean self-obsessed party animals," Mateo said quietly.

"Sure, but they didn't walk out on me like yours did," Buckley said to Jeff, then to Mateo he added, "And it's not like they ever rejected me for being gay. I feel like I don't have any right to complain."

"'Cause that's how you felt then," Mateo said. "Like if you complained or asked them to be parents for a minute or two, they'd lose interest and you'd be all alone. It might have been different if you'd had siblings, but you were on your own with them so you always took care of *them* and tried to be your funny, clever self to keep them entertained."

He felt more heat rush to his face and a tingling in his palms. And Jeff's patient nod only intensified the strange blend of self-consciousness that left him suddenly flushed and breathless. It was the same confusion he always felt when Mateo made him feel truly seen and loved. Now it was coming at him from two men, instead of one. He hungered for more, while feeling paralyzed by a fear he might say or do something to cut off the flow forever. So he resorted to his old standby. Deflection.

"So you're saying I'm entertaining? Even with my clothes on?" Buckley asked with a sheepish grin.

Jeff's low, commanding voice answered. "If you always put other people ahead of yourself, it can make it hard for someone to walk beside you."

The truth in the master sergeant's words, along with the subtle message that he wouldn't be put off by Buckley's humor, sent a tremor through him.

He thought about how he went over a year without confessing the depth of his fantasies and desires to his boyfriend, all while making Mateo's fantasies center stage.

But Jeff had made this observation without rising from his seat and making some excuse to leave the way his parents might have in a similar conversation, peppering him with distracted criticisms then leaving him on his own to figure out how to work his way through them.

Even better, when Mateo squeezed his knee, Jeff did the same, causing a matching sensation on the other side of his body. He felt a sudden desire to wilt into both of their arms at once.

"Okay," Buckley said quickly, "I go next since I just got asked. Mateo's up."

Jeff and Mateo cleared their throats, straightening in their seats like little boys trying to broadcast what good students they were.

"Dare," Mateo said.

Buckley slapped his lap with both hands. "Well, shit! There's goes my question."

"Yeah, but later you get to dare him to do whatever you want," Jeff added.

"Within reason," Mateo added. "Okay, I get to ask Jeff. Truth or dare?"

"Truth," Jeff answered.

"Have you ever been in love?"

Jeff hesitated, gazing into Mateo's eyes. He swallowed. The tension coursing up the sides of his powerfully built neck caused his veins to pop. "Yes," he finally said.

With you, Buckley thought. And maybe the men on either side of him were thinking it too, and that's why no one was saying anything. He thought it was a good thing, a beautiful thing, even. A thing that had made this crazy, amazing weekend possible, but it looked like the men on either side of it needed time to process this fact. And suddenly he did too.

Jeff swallowed. "More of a four p.m. tomorrow conversation, know what I mean?"

Which was as good as confirming Buckley's suspicion.

"Agreed," Mateo said softly.

The silence that passed over the table was deep and a little dark, and for a second, Buckley thought about cancelling the game. Then he realized he was feeling pressure on both knees, that under the table, both men were caressing him. Possessively. Hungrily. The feel of their combined touch, the sense of the three of them having formed a kind of chain together, felt as absolutely correct as the first time he'd kissed a boy.

"Alright, hit me again, Master Sergeant," Buckley said. But before Jeff could get a word out, Buckley added, "Dare!"

Jeff threw up his hands and smiled.

"Dare," Mateo said before Jeff could ask him anything.

"This is starting to feel rigged," Jeff said.

"Truth or dare?" Mateo asked him with a smile.

Giving them both a stern look, Jeff sank back into his chair. Their entrees arrived, allowing all of them to catch their breath.

"Truth," Jeff said after chewing his first bite of salmon.

"What's your biggest fear?" Mateo asked him.

"Failure. Not being prepared. I was the kid who always had nightmares about being in a play and no one had given me the script. Or I'd have to give a speech and I couldn't remember where it was written down. That kind of thing."

"Well, you're the most trained and competent guy I know, so it's paid off, I guess," Mateo said.

"But sometimes you can't prepare for the best things in life," Buckley said. "Besides, failure's relative."

Smiling, Jeff met his gaze. "Is that so, firecracker?"

"Sure. I mean, maybe you don't get one job you really want and then three weeks later you get another better job you didn't know to hope for. Or you find out the man you love can't bottom for you and you're all torn up about it, and then a year and a half later you find out his *amazing* boyfriend can take every inch you've got. It's all about the big picture."

Jeff exploded with laughter. "Is he always this cheerful?"

"Yep. It's part of what I love about him." Grinning, Mateo gripped the back of Buckley's neck gently. "That and his sweet pussy."

"*Babe!*"

Mateo and Jeff cackled as blood rushed to his cheeks.

"What?" Mateo asked, beaming. "It's hot that you like it called that. I love it."

Jeff said, "I'm just amazed there's something Buckley's afraid to say out loud."

"I'm not afraid? It's just…

"A very good pussy?" Jeff asked. This time, Mateo exploded with laughter.

Buckley slapped his napkin against his lap. "This is a hotel room conversation, not a lunchtime conversation." The truth was, he was so turned on at two commanding tops teasing him about how much they loved his ass, he thought he might slide off the table into a melting puddle of gay boy.

"Alright, Mister Truth Or Dare At The Table, we'll keep things nice and clean," Jeff said.

"Not clean. Honest."

A silence settled, but Mateo's smile hadn't left his face, and he was still gently stroking the back of Buckley's neck. "Well, I think we're being honest when we say if it gets you hot, then it gets us hot. And it's nothing to be ashamed of even if some douchebags in the past gave you some grief over it. Right, Braxton?"

"I second that," Jeff said, his voice a deep, thigh-tickling rumble.

If the table hadn't had a glass top, he might have sunk to the floor and started working on both of them underneath it.

"Alright, one last round, and we all have to take truth," Buckley said. "Deal?"

Chewing, both men nodded in turn. Jeff dabbed at his lips with his napkin and swallowed. "Buckley, what's the one thing you love most about Mateo?"

"He's kind. He never stops looking for ways to show me that he cares. In the beginning, I thought he might be an act, you know. The flowers and the gifts and the remembering our different anniversaries. I'd never had a man treat me like I was worth that amount of effort. That consistency. I've never had someone make me feel that valuable or special."

"Buckley," Mateo whispered, eyes glistening.

"Alright, Mateo," Buckley said, lacing his fingers through his under the table. "What do you love most about Jeff?"

Looking caught, as if he needed to remind himself of how far the three of them had come in such a short time, Mateo swallowed. "You mean aside from the fact that he saved my life?"

"Or in addition to," Buckley said.

Eyes on his old crew chief, Mateo said, "He's the kind of man I want to be. He's a leader without being a tyrant. The world was small until I met him. I always felt safe with him even before he saved my life."

Was Jeff about to cry? The tension in his jaw looked new. He was blinking rapidly. Fighting tears, maybe. He cleared his throat three times in quick succession. "Damn, Cano," he managed in a choked voice. "What are you trying to do to me here?"

"Alright, Master Sergeant," Mateo said. "Your turn. What do you love most about Buckley?"

Buckley looked up like a gun had gone off, genuinely shocked that Mateo had phrased the question about him and not himself. "Babe. I don't know if that's fair. We just met."

Undeterred, Jeff said, "He's strong. He doesn't get put off by other people's bullshit. Including mine. Last night when we were dancing together, when I couldn't scare him off with my hard-ass routine, I realized he was exactly who I'd want next to me if I was hurt. Exactly who I'd want holding my hand if I'd broken a bone."

Breathless, Buckley felt rooted to his chair, in thrall to the older man's sincerity and his gaze.

"And he's got a sweet fucking pussy," Jeff added.

Before he realized he'd thrown it at him, Buckley's napkin hit Jeff square in the chest. Grinning like the Joker, the man caught it in one hand. Mateo was laughing too. And so was Buckley. Maybe they could both feel it. Jeff Braxton was melting, softening. Smiling like he hadn't smiled the night before. Playing and teasing in a way that matched Buckley step for step.

"How would you know?" Mateo finally said. "You haven't tasted it yet."

"We're going to fix that real soon. But first, how about some beach time? Too bad I didn't bring my board."

Instantly, Jeff seemed to realize his mistake. His smile vanished, replaced by flaring nostrils and a tense jaw. Suddenly he was staring at Mateo like he was afraid the guy might fall apart right there.

Adam's apple bobbing, lips furrowed, Mateo stared down at his plate as he moved lettuce around with his fork.

Jeff looked like he was about to apologize for suggesting an afternoon of surfing to a man who'd almost drowned, but just then, Mateo jerked his head up and with a big beaming smile and said, "We could go swimming."

"You sure, babe?" Buckley asked.

Avoiding Buckley's eyes, Mateo shoveled a dangerously large bite of salad into his mouth. "Yeah, it'd be fun," he said between barn-animal-sized chews. "I mean, it's warm enough out, right?"

"I don't have a suit," Jeff said. "Maybe a hike or something. Do they have trails here?"

"I don't know if there're any on the property, but they've got some nearby," Buckley added. "I could see if there's a shuttle that—"

"No, no," Mateo said, shoveling food into his mouth. "You're my size. I think I brought two."

Jeff licked his lips and swallowed. "It's fine, Mateo. Don't worry about it."

"Come on. It's a beach resort. We can't *not* go to the beach."

"Yeah, but—"

"Wassa matter, Master Sergeant? Worried I'm going to try to squeeze you into a Speedo. They're board shorts. Promise. They won't make you look *gaaaaaaay.*"

Mateo smiled at both of them in turn, the kind of big, forced smile he gave people when he was nervous or hiding something. Then he announced he had to go to the bathroom and suddenly he was gone.

"I feel like a fucking idiot," Jeff said after he was gone.

"Don't."

"Has he even been surfing since the accident?"

Buckley shook his head. "Won't even get in a pool."

"And now he wants to go swimming in the ocean? What's going on here?"

"I think he's trying to impress you."

"Well, that's the last thing he needs to do."

"Who knows? Maybe it'll work. It's a weekend for trying new things, right?"

Jeff raised one eyebrow. "So you think we fucked him out of his PTSD?"

"You said that out loud, you know?"

Jeff winked at him. "I got a mouth that matches yours, firecracker."

"Maybe we keep quiet and follow his lead," Buckley finally said. "It's kind of the only choice I've had when it comes to this."

Under the table, Jeff caressed Buckley's knee. His eyes filled with an openness and compassion he'd yet to see in them, and suddenly he had no trouble understanding how this man had made Mateo feel safe even before he'd stopped his plummet into the ocean depths.

"How bad is it?" Jeff asked gently. "I mean, you took the dimmers out at the house. He won't even get in a pool. Is it coming up in other ways?"

Buckley hesitated. Mateo had begged him not to talk to his sister about it because she'd be all over him with holistic suggestions and supplements and phone numbers for LA psychics. With Mateo's parents out of the picture, that meant Buckley had discussed these issues with no one. "Elevators are out too. He's set off two fire alarms at school trying to take the stairs."

Closing his eyes, Jeff squeezed Buckley's knee tighter, as if absorbing this little piece of news like a blow. And Buckley felt a surge of relief. For the first time, he wasn't alone with his gnawing worry for the man he loved.

"Let's do like you said," Jeff finally said. "Let's follow his lead."

Mateo returned to the table, gesturing for the server to bring them the bill.

They did what they'd agreed to do and followed Mateo's lead all the way back to the villa. They changed hurriedly, Mateo talking a mile a minute about nothing in particular while Buckley and Jeff smiled and nodded and exchanged worried looks.

Sapphire Cove had a little crescent of private beach hemmed in by rocky cliff faces. The only land access was a twisting wooden staircase that descended the cliff from the lawn outside the hotel's ballrooms. Mateo took it several steps at a time, whooping and hollering like a sports fan entering a crowded arena before the big game. They didn't bother reserving any of the umbrella-shaded wooden loungers. Instead, they laid their towels down not too far from the surf's foamy edge. Buckley was relieved to see it was a relatively calm day. No real whitecaps, just gentle swells breaking with a soft whooshing sound close to the shore.

Still, the whole thing made him feel like he was being jerked along by a speeding train with no brakes, even though everything about this felt rushed and wrong. Then Mateo ran into the ocean, Jeff following. Buckley did the same, diving under as soon as the water came up to his waist. When he broke the surface, he saw Mateo swimming a few yards ahead. Treading water now, his boyfriend turned toward them, smiling as big as he had during their race to the beach. For a second, Buckley thought it would work. That Jeff's return and their hours of passion had healed Mateo's paralyzing fear of the place he'd once loved—the ocean.

Then he was gone.

Buckley stood suddenly, surprised to find the water only waist deep. *"Mateo!"* His voice betrayed the fear he'd been fighting ever since they'd left the brunch table. Jeff was a few yards away, staring back at the shore.

Shoulders slumped, head slightly bowed, Mateo was emerging from the water, making a beeline for their stuff. He toweled himself off, movements frenzied, more dabs than swipes. Like the droplets of water were hurting his skin.

"Babe?" Buckley called after him as he pursued. He heard the splashes of Jeff moving through the water next to him.

"I'm fine." Mateo's croak didn't sound remotely fine.

But he wouldn't look at them and his nostrils were flaring, his lips parted with heavy breaths that lifted his back.

"You two have fun," he said quickly. "I'm gonna…go up to the room and…"

"Hey, Cano. Maybe we sit for a bit and catch our breath," Jeff asked.

"No, I'm going up. It's fine." He sounded like the Mateo he'd first met, bashful and quiet but also constantly tense. He'd tried to pole vault over his worst fear and been knocked backward in an instant, and all Buckley wanted to do was throw his arms around him. But Mateo was already walking across the sand in his flip-flops, one arm raised behind him as if he was trying to bid them good-bye and freeze them in place with the same gesture.

His vision blurred. By the time Mateo was halfway up the steps, he was blinking back tears.

"I hate this," he whispered. "I wish he'd get angry, you know? Or lash out. But all he does is get so hurt and embarrassed, and it breaks my heart every time. I mean, the ocean's one thing, but he had a job interview with a private security firm in Irvine a few weeks ago. It was on the seventh floor, and the building wouldn't let him take the stairs. He was so humiliated he didn't go. Never told them why, either. That's not like him at all, but what's he gonna do? Tell a security company he's too afraid to ride an elevator?"

"Is he talking to anyone? Any therapists?"

"I've tried three. One was this rapid eye movement therapy clinic. He called it science fiction stuff, but it's shown results with trauma victims. He kept bailing on the first appointment. The other two were on his insurance plan, talk therapy. He bailed after two sessions with each. Said it was too touchy feely."

"Has he talked to any of his old Marine friends about this?"

Buckley shook his head. Then he felt Jeff take his hand.

"Come on," the older man said, and in a tone that brooked no argument. "Let's go. I've got this."

11

Mateo's hands were still shaking as he stumbled into the villa's spacious walk-in shower.

In an instant, the ocean had gone from feeling like a refreshing balm to a freezing vise grip that might drag him under and crush him. The shower's warm spray made that moment of paralyzing panic feel a little bit further away, but fear still thrummed inside his bones.

He'd ruined everything. Sent their wild weekend spinning down the drain, all because he'd wanted to be strong in front of Jeff.

After he dried himself off, he went for the bottle of champagne they hadn't touched the night before, feeling like the sweaty warmth of his fingers against the glass ruined this special gift as well. It had been intended for celebration and romance. Now he was fishing it out of a bucket of melted ice and gulping a glass of its lukewarm contents like it was medicine.

A shame spiral, that's what he was in.

One of the therapists, the one he'd liked the better of the two, had taught him the term. But he'd given up on her after she asked him to keep a daily log of when his memories of the accident were the worst. In the moment, he'd nodded and agreed. But his stomach had twisted at the thought, and he'd known right then he'd never set foot in her office again. He couldn't decide what was worse—reliving his near drowning or admitting how frequently he was overpowered by flashbacks.

The bathroom, for some reason, felt safe. Maybe because he could lock the door if Buckley and Jeff came back. But he forgot to and the next thing he knew, he was sitting on the tile floor, back resting against the tub, staring down at the nearly empty flute in his hands.

He heard the villa's entry door open. Jeff gently called his name. A dull voice inside his head told him to get up and lock himself in the bathroom. Fake sick. Food poisoning. Whatever. Anything but this. Anything but fear.

But before he could will himself to move, they were standing in the bathroom door, towering over him, it seemed. The expressions on their faces were full of loving concern, but their height made him feel judged. When they sank to the floor on either side of him, the tears he'd been fighting tensed his jaw and blurred his vision. They were coming down to his level, taking his hands gently, bringing their warmth to him, making the tile floor and the side of the tub his back rested against feel less cold all of a sudden.

"You trying to impress me, buddy?" Jeff asked softly. "You think I don't know how hard it was, what you went through? I was down there with you. It was almost lights-out for both of us. You don't shake that kinda thing off like a bad cold."

"It was a fucking training accident. It's not like it was combat, you know?"

"The Osprey's killed fifty-seven Marines in twenty-three years. They had to ground the whole fleet for months before it was good to fly again. Don't think for one damn minute what you went through is any less than someone who had to stare down an IED after it blew."

There it was. Jeff had hit a bull's-eye—he wasn't dealing with his PTSD because he thought it was somehow less serious than the gnarly shit Marines like Jeff had been through in combat.

"What you *both* went through," Buckley said softly.

Jeff nodded. "I'm going to tell you what they told me after I got back from my first deployment. There's PTSD and then there's what you tell yourself about PTSD. Sometimes that second thing hurts a lot worse."

"What hurts is not living up to your standards."

"*My* standards?" Jeff sounded like someone had knocked the wind out of him. He pulled Mateo close with one arm around his shoulders. Mateo wanted to keep his head up, maybe bring their lips together, but he was still too embarrassed, and so the man's lips grazed his forehead instead. "You're not my Marine anymore, Cano.

You're moving on, trying new things. I don't need you combat ready. I need you happy. I need you here with us. And I sure as hell don't need you plowing headfirst into the ocean before you're ready. I would've gone anywhere you wanted me to on dry land today. I still will."

When Jeff kissed his forehead, Mateo felt the cold of the sea leave his bones at last. "I'm putting Buckley through hell."

Shaking his head, Buckley tightened his grip on Mateo's hand. "You're not, baby. I just hate seeing you like this."

"You're always so helpful and you're always coming up with ideas on how to deal with this and I'm always bailing or shooting it down."

Buckley swallowed and looked to Jeff.

"It's hard to talk about this kind of stuff with people who haven't been through it," Jeff said. "I've got a guy. Really good therapist, but he's former enlisted. He's down by me but he does weekend sessions, and your insurance should cover it." Jeff tightened his grip on the back of Mateo's neck. "This guy, he was the first I could sit with. Open up to." He looked to Buckley. "I'm sure the other therapists were fine, but there's a shift that happens when you're talking with someone who's served. I can't describe it. But it's important. A big part of what you're dealing with is self-judgment. This guy, he's never made me feel judged."

Mateo nodded. "I'll do it."

"That's right. You'll do at least five sessions. If money's an issue, I'll help you out. But you're not bailing before five."

"Or else what?" Mateo looked into Jeff's eyes for the first time since they'd all ended up on the bathroom floor together.

Jeff smiled. "Or else you're never going to get to see me fuck your boyfriend."

Mateo huffed with laughter. "That sounds like cruel and unusual punishment."

"I second that," Buckley said.

It was the first time he could remember crying in front of the man he'd worshiped.

It was certainly the first time, after baring his soul to him, that their lips had met.

He felt Buckley's breath against the other side of his neck. When his mouth moved to his it was like one kiss seamlessly flowing into the other.

Before Buckley, before this moment, his life had been full of people he felt he had to please or impress. For the first time, he felt like he was in the presence of two men who could put him back together again. They started by guiding him to the bed.

12

Once Mateo's breaths turned slow and even, Jeff slipped out of bed and took a quick shower. Bringing the smell of the ocean to bed with him might trigger a flashback for the man in their care.

When he returned, Buckley was sliding from the sheets, no doubt getting ready to do the same.

Was the guy avoiding his eyes as he moved past him toward the bathroom?

As he snuggled against Mateo again, Jeff found himself turning this worry over in his head, even as he felt comforted by the warmth of the man next to him, who was out cold, felled by the adrenaline crash that follows a panic attack.

Quietly, Buckley returned to bed. When his hand found one of Jeff's across Mateo's body, Jeff's anxiety left him and soon he was sleeping so deeply he wasn't sure if the sounds that eventually roused him were echoes of a dream. By the time he sat up in bed, he was alone with Mateo, the memory of Buckley shifting the sheets, tapping the screen of his phone, quietly sliding on clothes, coming to him out of sequence.

He pushed back the drape. No sign of him on the tiny balcony. He searched for a note. There wasn't one. No text on his phone either.

His heart dropped. The muscles in his upper back felt like a solid, aching plate.

He'd overstepped. He should have talked over his suggestions with Buckley first, given him a chance to play a role. Buckley was Mateo's boyfriend, after all. And what was Jeff? That was a four p.m.

tomorrow conversation for sure, but in the meantime, he shouldn't have swept in all Marine Corps rescue-hero like, making Buckley feel like his past efforts had been weak failures.

He pulled on some of Mateo's clothes, donned a pair of flip-flops, and headed out in search of Buckley.

In the hotel's lobby, he caught sight of him. Exactly as Jeff had feared, he was heading for the motor court, phone in hand. A total reverse of how they'd first met the night before.

"Yeah, that's not how we're handling this," Jeff barked.

At the sound of his voice, Buckley spun. Jeff closed the distance between them.

"We made a deal. Four p.m. tomorrow we talk about the tough stuff. So if what I did is something we need to talk about, then we talk about it then. But you're not going anywhere, firecracker."

"What you *did?*" Buckley asked.

Buckley's phone let out a chime at the same moment a dirt-splotched Toyota Prius pulled into the motor court behind him, looking out of place among the other black SUVs and idling hotel sedan cars.

"You basically put this whole thing together. So you're going to see it through with the two of us. You don't get to hop in an Uber and hightail it out of here the minute things get rough."

The Prius came to a halt behind Buckley. He turned to it, but he didn't go for the back door. Instead, the driver—a young woman with short, flame-red hair and a tattoo of a slender rosebush crawling up one side of her neck—hopped out, carrying a plastic bag with a CVS logo on it. She handed Buckley the bag, then her eyes met Jeff's and she said, "You boys have fun."

As the Prius pulled off, Buckley approached him. His head was bowed, and he was fighting laughter. He held the bag open so Jeff could see its contents. "She wasn't an Uber. She was an Instacart driver."

Condoms. Buckley had ordered them some condoms on his phone.

"A rather familiar one if you ask me." Feeling his cheeks flame, Jeff took the bag from Buckley's hands, as if that, and his ornery deflection, would somehow make this moment less awkward.

"What was that about *hightailing it outta here*, Master Sergeant?" Buckley asked.

"I thought we agreed to lose the rank thing."

"Sorry, but that was definitely a master sergeant moment. An awkward one for sure, but still…"

"And no making fun of my accent."

"Oh, I'm not making fun. Believe me. Your accent makes me want to ride you like a horse. Hence the…" Buckley gently batted the CVS bag now hanging from Jeff's hand. "By your request, remember?"

"You know the hotel's got a romance kit in the wet bar," Jeff said, even though he was pretty sure he should stop talking for at least a few minutes.

"It's only got two, though." Buckley smiled and waggled his eyebrows.

Feeling both embarrassed and aroused, Jeff turned. "Let's head back to the room."

"Yes, *sir*," Buckley answered with what sounded like delight in his voice.

Neither of them spoke until they'd entered the broad lawn that lay between the hotel's main building and the first row of terraced villas.

"So maybe this is a tomorrow conversation, but I'm thinking this little moment was a bit of projection." Buckley still sounded thoroughly amused.

"Oh yeah?"

"Yeah. It sounds like a lot of people have walked out on you. Maybe you protect yourself sometimes by walking out first."

Jeff froze, turned to face the boy who drove him wild in every definition of the word. "Like I did with Mateo, you mean."

"Maybe." His voice was soft, his eyes slightly downcoast. Confident, strutting Buckley was trying to be gentle with Jeff's heart. And his past.

"On the way up from the beach, I should have told you what I was going to say. We could have talked strategy. Made it sound like it was your idea too."

"Why would I need it to be my idea? You think I brought you back into his life for that? Because I *don't* want him to have your wisdom and experience?"

"I guess not."

At first, Jeff thought the heat on the side of his face was his own embarrassment. Then he opened his eyes and saw Buckley had rested one hand there.

"I like this part, Jeff," he whispered. Not master sergeant, but his name, which meant Buckley wanted him to hear these words down to his bones. "You and me, trying to make his life better. Together. I like it as much as everything else we've been doing."

"I like it too," Jeff said.

Buckley's lips parted, and for a few head-spinning seconds Jeff thought they might kiss right there. But instead, Buckley took his hand and pulled him gently back inside the lobby. "Come on. We don't want Mateo to wake up alone."

Mateo was still sleeping when they returned to the villa, but he'd shifted position in bed and was lying on his back, the sheet halfway down his chest, suggesting he'd stirred in their absence. Buckley set the bag down on the dresser, then crawled across the bed until his mouth was inches above Mateo's. He caressed the side of his face gently. Mateo's dark eyelashes fluttered. Their lips met gently, then Mateo curved one arm around Buckley's back, driving their bodies together as he let out a sleepy, satisfied groan.

It thrilled Jeff, observing this moment of intimacy between them. Their easy confidence with each other's bodies. Maybe he had more of a voyeuristic streak than he'd realized. But they weren't acting as if he wasn't there. They were acting as if his presence were natural, fated, and nothing needed to be held back in front of him.

"Where'd you guys go?" Mateo asked, sounding groggy.

"Jeff had a moment."

"I *didn't* have a moment."

"He had a moment."

Mateo's sleepy eyes met Jeff's. "What kinda moment?"

"He thought I got jealous and walked out."

Brow furrowed, Mateo looked up at his boyfriend. "Did you?"

"Nope. I went to get condoms so he could fuck me. A lot."

Jeff shook his head. "I swear to God, kid. Your mouth…"

"Now he feels kinda silly. But it's okay." Buckley gently rolled over onto his back, scooting down Mateo's body so the man could embrace him from behind. "I'm still going to let him fuck me. If it's alright with my boyfriend, that is."

"You two…" Jeff whispered. The aftereffects of the possessive anger he'd felt at the sight of Buckley walking toward the motor court had sharpened his desire. Made him feel like the guy had been snatched away and given back.

"We three," Buckley whispered in response, his smile fading into a look more intent, hypnotic. A look that made Jeff feel like he was floating up out of his skin, preparing to descend upon the two men before him like a cloud of pure force, pure want.

"That's all well and good," Mateo said. "But I believe we've got some dares in the bank."

<h1 style="text-align:center">13</h1>

Sprawled naked across the comforter, Buckley tried not to writhe in frustration over the fact that neither of the men near him on the bed would touch him. Yet.

According to their unofficial tally, Mateo had banked two dares, one from Jeff and one from Buckley. Buckley had banked only one, and it was from Jeff. But Mateo was still recovering from their aborted swim, so they'd decided Buckley would go first. Which was why he was now ass up and face down, gooseflesh prickling his skin as he anticipated the sweet torture to come.

Carefully, gently, Jeff placed a row of small plastic toiletry bottles down Buckley's spine. Six in all, the set from the tub and the set from the walk-in shower.

"Remind me how this works again?"

Mateo, who was propped against the headboard in nothing but a pair of white boxers, watched their setup routine with a hungry look in his eyes. "Jeff is going to eat your ass to the best of his abilities. You have to stay completely still the whole time. Knock over one of the bottles and he stops. Then you have to sit up, look me dead in the eye, and describe one of the sexual fantasies you've been keeping secret for a year. In explicit, explicit detail."

"Secret is such a…strong word. All I did was make yours front and center. Doesn't that make me a good, generous boyfriend?"

"No back talk, firecracker." Jeff punctuated his point by giving one of Buckley's bare ass cheeks a little, teasing peck.

Jesus, this was going to be hard. He'd seen firsthand what the older man's talented tongue could do. Buckley was way more sensitive down there than Mateo was. Nothing drove him over a wall faster than a good rim job.

He sighed into the sheets. "Fine."

Jeff started with a slow, confident caress of both of Buckley's cheeks. Then he gently nuzzled his nose into Buckley's ass crack. Small, intimate, teasing, these little gestures sent blood thundering through Buckley's veins. They said *I am utterly at home here and will stay down here as long as you let me.* Experienced as he was, he didn't make the mistake of kneading his ass like it was bread dough, either. Instead, he parted Buckley's cheeks, breathing gently against his quivering hole, leaving Buckley to imagine the intent, focused look on the man's face as he surveyed the landscape he was about to ravage.

Jeff let out a throaty groan. "This is good fucking pussy."

"Cheating!" Buckley cried.

Laughing, Mateo, said, "He's right, man. We said no dirty talk. Just tongue action."

"Fine," Jeff growled, then gave Buckley a little bite on one cheek to punish him.

The first stroke was long and wet and wide. And perfect. Absolutely perfect, and Buckley had no choice but to screw his eyes shut, breathing hard and fast through his nostrils. His reflex was to bend his knees, give Jeff more ready access, but the rules said he had to stay completely still. It was hard, so hard. And this was merely the intro, he was sure. Jeff was preparing the field, getting it nice and slick so that his wilder tongue movements would slip and slide and flicker with less friction.

"You like that, *papi*?"

"Cheating," Buckley whispered through hissing, teeth-clenched breaths.

"Sorry." It sounded like Mateo was smiling, but Buckley couldn't look up.

Jeff unleashed a head-spinning two step on Buckley's ass—mad, focused flickers right at Buckley's hole followed by long wet swipes to keep the whole area slick. One round, then another. Halfway through the third, bolts of pleasure shot up his spine. In his mind's eye, he saw himself driving his ass up and back into Jeff's working tongue like a little bitch in heat. Which was exactly how he felt.

Two of the bottles on his lower back went over and slid to the bed. "Dammit."

When Jeff backed off Buckley's ass, it felt like all the air in the room was departing with him. Mateo collected the little bottles that were still standing.

"Alright," Jeff said with a cocky grin. "Let's hear one."

Buckley sat up, sank back onto his haunches. He was nervous. But he was also determined to dive into this challenge headfirst, no looking back.

"Okay, so I go off to Vegas with some friends. I promise you I won't gamble, but I do, and I lose a bunch of our money. When I come home and tell you, you're trying to keep it together but I can also tell you're pissed. Then you tell me I have to earn the money back somehow..."

"How?" Mateo asked.

"You tie me naked to the bed and then you invite a bunch of friends over and you charge them to fuck me one by one."

Jeff's throaty grunt and eager smile suggested he was trying not to holler with horny delight. Mateo's eyes were aflame.

"And all your friends look like Jeff," Buckley added, batting his eyelashes.

Mateo swallowed, chewed his bottom lip.

"Actually, one or two look like your cousin Antonio."

"Antonio's a tool."

"Yes, but he's a dirty, hot tool. And I didn't say he comes over for brunch. He comes over to rail me with all your other buddies while you make money off my ass like it's a betting table. Look, do you want to hear my fantasies or not?"

Laughing in his throat, Mateo chewed his lower lip. Answer enough.

Buckley settled down onto the bed, chest first and ass up once more. He patted his back. "Time for round two."

Mateo lined up the little bottles again, then came the magical feel of Jeff's hands cupping his cheeks, his first few breaths tickling his hole.

His entire body wanted to bend and dance to the waves of pleasure Jeff sent through him, but he held still. Like dirty talk, finger fucking was out, but Jeff was allowed to use his fingertips to trace little paths of pleasure along his crack and across his cheeks to accompany the work of his tongue. Within another minute or two, the room seemed to slip away. The bedding beneath him felt as hot as his own skin. He felt exposed, but also owned and cherished all in one dizzying, breathless moment.

This time, a bottle near the top of his spine went down like an injured soldier.

This time, rising to his knees took ten times the effort, given the blissful state to which Jeff had just sent him.

It took a few deep breaths for him to meet his boyfriend's expectant gaze. When he did, he saw Mateo had pushed his boxers down his thick, smooth thighs and was slowly stroking himself. It was another fight, not taking his boyfriend into his mouth when he saw the slick thread of pre-cum glistening along his shaft, especially given the delicious combo of his smug expression and the brazen way he stroked himself. Meanwhile, Jeff stood next to the bed, as the head of his hard cock poked above the waistband of his briefs.

"Let's hear another one, *papi*." Mateo's voice sounded gravelly and low.

"You take me to a Marine Corps ball with a bunch of your old friends and everyone's drinking and having a good time, and then you take me into the bathroom where a bunch of them are waiting for us. And you tell me you've told them all what a good little cocksucker I am, so you shove me to my knees and make me suck them while they're all in their dress blues, one after the other." Buckley looked to Jeff. "Call me a chaser again and I'll rip off your nuts."

"Do the friends all look like me this time too?" Jeff asked.

"Pretty much, yeah."

Jeff smiled. "Then I'll just say you've got good taste."

"Cocky bastard."

Jeff winked at him. That wink, Buckley realized, was gaining an enormous amount of power over him.

They returned to position.

Jeff started leisurely and slow this time, adding little nibbles to the inside of Buckley's cheeks. Then, out of nowhere, punching jabs that caused Buckley to clench his teeth and groan.

A mistake.

He should have stayed quiet. Now he'd let Jeff know his strategy was working. He went silent again. Lost track of time. Jeff's tongue traveled from the bulge his balls made against the mattress to the very top of his crack. In the silence, Jeff grunted, a small, hungry sound that made clear how much growing evidence of his desire he was holding back so he could focus on his work.

That did it. Buckley's hips tensed, and he felt a bottle in the small of his back go over sideways.

When Buckley rose to his knees again, he found Mateo stroking himself, eyes lust glazed, cock slick with pre-cum under his working hand.

"What if I'm out?" Buckley asked.

"I doubt that, firecracker," Jeff said as he caught his breath.

"I think you're afraid of this one," Mateo said quietly. "And you shouldn't be. You don't have to be afraid of anything when it comes to me."

"We're getting married and…you go off to have your bachelor party and I sneak around and follow you guys because I'm afraid you're going to cheat."

"Afraid?" Jeff asked.

Buckley gave him a dirty look, which made the man lift his eyebrows. "Fine. I'm not afraid. I just want to watch you do it. So you and your friends are at this big strip club, all boys. And you go back to one of the champagne rooms for a private dance, and I'm watching through the doorway as this hot stripper gyrates all over you and then…you just can't help yourself anymore."

"What do I do?" Mateo asked, voice raw with hunger.

"You reach out and you grab his ass and you just dive in, tongue first. And I'm standing there in the shadows, stroking my cock while I watch you. And then you're fucking him. And it's the most beautiful thing I've ever seen. You fucking him. You being wild and free and completely unbidden. And I should feel hurt and betrayed, but instead I'm feeling like I'm seeing every inch of you, every side of you. Like I'm getting more of you than I ever have before. Then suddenly one of your friends catches me and drags me into the room. And you don't stop fucking the stripper. You order your friends to start taking turns on me so you don't have to stop."

Slowly, Mateo rose up on his haunches, closing the distance between them. Gently he gripped Buckley's chin in one hand. His nostrils were flaring and his chest was rising and falling with deep, hungry breaths.

"I'm starting to notice a trend," he said.

"Oh yeah?"

"In each one, you belong to me."

Buckley nodded. "And I'm yours to share with whoever you want."

Mateo tightened his grip on Buckley's chin. "Jeff?"

"Yes, Mateo."

"Fuck our boy's pussy."

As he heard the rip of the condom wrapper and the pop of the lube bottle's cap, he felt himself go boneless. Then he was turned onto his back. He wasn't sure which man had done it, only that he was suddenly gazing up at the hypnotizing intensity of Jeff's expression, the sight of a man whose every muscle, whose every inch, was being commanded by desire for what he wanted most.

Buckley had never felt more open, more hungry, in his life.

Mateo was gifted downstairs. Jeff was bigger, and when he settled into him the head of his cock slid across Buckley's prostate with smooth force. The men above him saw his cock jerk in response and let out satisfied grunts.

Mateo gently guided his pre-cum-weeping cock into Buckley's eager, yawning mouth.

Buckley had been spit roasted before, but never like this. He'd never felt this utterly married to cock.

Jeff's long, slow strokes were sweet torture, a sign he'd sensed how well his cock's size and shape were pegging Buckley's special spot. And Mateo wasn't simply fucking his mouth. He was slowly spreading his pre-cum across Buckley's lips. Coating him, anointing him. It wasn't a ravaging, but it was slow and steady and determined. And focused. On him and only him. He felt things he rarely felt but always craved. Picked, special, *first*.

"Our boy's a hungry slut, Mateo," Jeff grunted between thrusts. "A hungry little poly slut."

Poly. He knew the term but had never applied it to himself before. And something about Jeff's use of it now—it wasn't exactly the stuff of bargain-basement dirty talk—made him feel more claimed. A diagnosis driven not by judgment, but by their mutual, building desire.

Mateo shifted to his knees next to Buckley's head, fucking his mouth with long, slow strokes. Head turned to one side, Buckley devoured each stroke with such suckling hunger he went numb to the growing strain in his neck until it turned into a brief, sharp stab. When he saw Buckley wince, Jeff shifted forward, lifting him up onto all fours.

Gripping his hips, Jeff started taking him from behind. Mateo's cock was filling his throat. He went from feeling boneless to fleshless, like his body was an illusion and he'd become nothing but incandescent energy thrown off in waves by the percussive shocks of the cocks pounding him from both ends. He'd lost all sense of where he ended and where Jeff and Mateo began. As experienced as he was, he'd never felt anything like this before. And when he reached down and began stroking himself, he thought his cock might explode in his hand.

Jeff wailed. It was a terrifying sound at first, easy to mistake for pain or terror. He'd seen the man come that morning. The event had been focused and fierce. This sound was different, raw and animalistic and wild. Wet heat filled the condom. The man's powerful thrusts stuttered then jerked. He was emptying hard and fast inside of him, his wails turning into a series of *Ohs* that sounded like he was pleading with something, some higher power. Begging for his life, his sanity. It was the wild sounds of an impeccably controlled man flying apart in the face of a satisfaction, a *connection*, that had overwhelmed him.

Like a wave, it hit Buckley next.

He bellowed, thighs shuddering so hard as he stroked himself he thought he might go over sideways off his bent knees. Amidst this melee of trembling lust, the steadiness of Mateo's smooth, throat-filling strokes sent him firmly over the edge.

It was like the first time he'd ever come, when the thunder and sweep of the sensations were so overwhelming and new, he wasn't quite sure what he'd done to himself at first.

Suddenly their arms were around him. They sank to the comforter together. Their quick transition from aggressive topping to tender embraces and gentle kisses told him they could feel how intense, how *serious*, Buckley's orgasm had been.

He thought, for a second, that these feelings might kill him. That his heart was about to stop. They were that intense. But in the same instant, he was exhilarated to know he would die happier than he'd ever been before.

Then he became more aware of the dual embrace in which he was tangled. Mateo's mouth against the back of his neck, then he was leaving gentle, reverential kisses on his forehead. A breathy silence fell. When Buckley opened his eyes, he saw Mateo looking past him.

Slowly, Buckley rolled onto his back.

Next to them Jeff looked like a sated warrior, exhausted by a post-victory bacchanal, hair-dusted chest rising and falling from his deep breaths, one forearm draped across his forehead, eyes closed, nostrils flaring.

Overwhelmed.

Overcome.

Buckley snuggled against him, tracing his fingers gently across his chest, afraid, for a moment, that Jeff might push him away. Instead, Jeff gripped Buckley's hand and brought it to his lips, kissed it gently, then held it against his chest. But the man couldn't seem to open his eyes. Like his grip on Buckley's hand was a way of reminding himself he was still real, still made of flesh and bone.

There'd been moments like this with Mateo in the beginning, when they'd opened up a part of him so deep and untouched that they'd had to lie there in silence for a while afterward, Buckley fearing he might have taken his boyfriend too far down a new and unpaved road. Realizing that being penetrated and filled wasn't the only path to a man's undoing. Had they somehow done the same to Jeff? Given the man's experience, the prospect seemed both implausible and wonderful.

You could fuck a top from the bottom. You could drain him of all resistance and good sense if you played your ass right. He'd learned that with Mateo, and now he'd done it with Jeff.

Finally, Jeff turned his head toward them, glassy-eyed, spent, like someone rousing from a long sleep to find himself pleasantly surprised by his bed partners.

"Sorry about that, guys." His polite word choice didn't match his winded tone. "I kind of lost it there for a sec."

"Or you found it."

It was Mateo who'd said it, but Buckley had been thinking almost exactly the same thing, so he smiled.

Jeff wasn't smiling. But he was gazing back at them both with something in his eyes that looked like eagerness edged with fear.

Found it.

Found *them.*

We're never going to make it until four p.m. tomorrow, Buckley thought.

Jeff's gaze suggested a speech was coming, one with more emotion than stern instructions. The man's shell had been cracking ever since their first kiss, a kiss Mateo had commanded. But the sounds he'd made suggested the shell might have split down the center. And for good.

Buckley, drained of all energy seconds before, felt his heart race.

Embracing him from behind, Mateo went very still.

"So," Jeff finally said, "what's for dinner, boys?"

Relief and disappointment in one.

They had either broken something or built something entirely new.

Tomorrow they would find out.

14

In the battle that consumed their last night at Sapphire Cove, Mateo resolved to stay neutral. That way he could sit back and savor the sights and sounds of the two men he loved most as they passionately debated which was the better franchise—*Star Wars* or *Star Trek.*

While asserting that *Rogue One* was one of the greatest movies of all time, Jeff used his typical, precise hand gestures and spoke with a low, focused intensity that sent chills up Mateo's spine. Buckley, on the other hand, sat upright on the edge of the bed, looking bright-eyed and eager—and utterly kissable—as he delivered a perky lecture on how *Star Trek IV: The Voyage Home* was a historically significant film that offered up a warm-hearted exploration of America's Cold War anxieties at the end of the Reagan era.

The last line sounded lifted from someone's blog, but Mateo thought that only made the little sermon more adorable.

Jeff listened intently, then once Buckley was done, he nodded a few times and said, "Your boyhood love of humpback whales does not a good movie make, firecracker."

Unleashing a burst of whale song that also sounded like a warlike cry, Buckley lunged. Suddenly the two men were cackling as they wrestled on the bed. Mateo joined in, and a few seconds later Buckley was pinned and the two of them were lightly spanking his creamy white cheeks until they turned rosy, which, of course, gave Mateo an immediate, raging hard-on, reminding them all that he hadn't come during their earlier session.

It was heaven, lying back on the comforters while they lathered him with hungry attention. When they finished him off, the bliss coursed through him in several pulsing waves that twisted his legs against the sheets, then he watched, breathless, as Buckley passed his still seed-slick cock from his own mouth to Jeff's, allowing the older man to suck up all the pearly threads Buckley had missed.

Once he'd caught his breath, Mateo said, "Sorry, but House Atreides can beat all the starship and stormtrooper ass you throw at it."

"Help," Buckley muttered into the pillow, "my boyfriend's a Duniac."

More laughter, more champagne, a dinner from room service Jeff insisted on putting on his card, then a deep, dreamless sleep more contented than any he could remember.

Until it was interrupted by a ringing phone.

Mateo's eyes popped open to a sundrenched room and the sudden, heavy realization that today was the day this blissful, magical weekend came to an end.

The call was from room service. Buckley's old friend, the general manager, was offering them a free breakfast, but the kitchen would be turning over to the lunch menu in half an hour.

My God, Mateo realized. They'd slept until ten.

He alerted the men in bed, then headed for the shower.

When he emerged, Buckley was using the in-room coffeemaker and Jeff was seated on the edge of the bed, scrolling through his phone, clearly waiting for his turn under the spray. The mood was quiet. Disconnected. Tense with morning-after vibes.

With a polite smile, Jeff darted past him into the bathroom.

Once he'd pulled on jeans and a T-shirt, Mateo sidled up to Buckley at the coffeemaker and embraced him from behind. Buckley wilted into him. Together they listened to the coffeemaker's gurgle competing with the rush of the shower.

A short while later, Jeff emerged, wrapped in a towel. "Buckley, you're up." Brusque, officious. Like they were all on base.

When his boyfriend headed past Jeff with little more than a glancing touch on the small of the man's back, Mateo's doubt turned to dread. Was this really going to come to an end that quickly? Or was he reading too deeply into their smallest gestures because he was nervous as hell about their meeting that afternoon?

"Got another outfit for me?" Jeff asked.

Mateo nodded and went to his weekend bag. He was about to hand the folded jeans and a polo shirt to Jeff when his muscles all seemed to freeze in one instant. "Listen," he started, but he wasn't sure what he was going to say. Maybe something about moving up their big discussion so it wouldn't be hanging over their heads all day. Then the villa's doorbell rang, startling them both. Breakfast had arrived.

After giving the waiter a cash tip, they transferred the plates to the little dining table. In distracted silence, the three of them scarfed down their breakfasts, the laughter and ocean sounds drifting in through the open deck door like some radio transmission from the other side of the world.

Jeff finally broke the silence with, "You were saying?"

It took Mateo a second to realize the man was talking to him.

Maybe twenty minutes had passed since he'd first started trying to put his thoughts together while handing Jeff a change of clothes, and the man was acting as if it had only been seconds ago.

Jesus, we're freaked.

"I can't remember." That was a lie. He could totally remember. Moving the meeting up, that's what he'd been about to suggest. Why was he too nervous to suggest it now?

Silence descended again.

Jeff scarfed down his last bite of eggs Benedict and pushed the plate back. "Okay, here's the plan." For a second, Mateo thought his old crew chief was about to start the big talk right there, and his heart raced from a blend of anxiety and relief. "Checkout time's at four, right?" Buckley nodded. "We should sit down and talk this out at two then. Fine. So I need a few hours to put my thoughts together before then. Do y'all know if this place has a business center?"

Buckley furrowed his brow. "I think so. Why?"

"This meeting needs an agenda."

"Like a *written* agenda?" Buckley asked, sounding shocked.

Jeff nodded, folding his napkin as he rose to his feet. "I prefer to put my thoughts in writing. Helps me get clear about stuff."

"Okay, but is it fine if I don't?" Buckley said.

Jeff nodded. "Y'all do what you need to do. Before the meeting, I mean. At around two, I'll meet you guys back here and we'll talk through all this."

Before he could stop himself, Mateo rose to his feet. "That's hours from now. You're just going to wander around by yourself?"

"I'm going to the business center. That's all." Mateo must have looked doubtful. "And y'all can take the time to get on the same page about this."

"Whatever we have to say about this we should all say in front of each other."

Jeff seemed shocked. He clearly wasn't used to being bossed around by one of his old junior Marines. Or bossed around at all. But wasn't that what this entire weekend had been about? Seeing new sides of each other? He wasn't the Mateo Jeff had known a year and a half ago. If he'd been as confident and in touch with his sexuality back then, maybe their weekend in San Diego would have resulted in something like this. Something that felt like it had potential. But that wouldn't have been possible because he hadn't met Buckley yet. And it was Buckley who made this possible, Buckley who had brought him and Jeff together in ways they'd never connected before. And maybe he should say all of this right now, right here.

But that might catch Buckley off guard.

The three of them had made a plan, an agreement, and they should stick to it.

"I'm not going anywhere except the business center, Cano. I promise."

But he left without kissing either of them good-bye.

Even worse, he was back to calling Mateo by his last name.

As he watched Jeff leave, Mateo felt Buckley's hand close around his. He brought it to his lips and kissed Buckley's fingers, but he couldn't tear his eyes away from the heavy door that had swung shut.

"How about a walk, babe?"

Mateo nodded.

The staircase that led to all the villa entry doors descended downhill toward a paved pathway with a stunning view south down the coast. It felt like one of the resort's more secret spots. The folks who wandered the walkway's main portion outside the hotel's ballrooms probably assumed the pathway's sudden sharp turn in front of the villas meant it was a space exclusively reserved for villa guests.

The two of them leaned against a ranch-style fence that looked solid and stylized, the kind of recreation-rustic you'd find in an amusement park. Beyond, ice plant formed a heavy pelt along the top of the bluff. The insides of its thick green leaves were rose colored, like they were blushing at everything that had happened just uphill that weekend in villa 6E.

"A written agenda." Buckley laughed under his breath. "Guess I should have seen that one coming." Mateo smiled, but he was still rattled by how much his fear had taken control of him. Buckley curved an arm around him and pulled him close. "Well, should we get on the same page like he said?"

Mateo turned to him. "I'm not sure where to start."

"Start with what scares you the most. I promise to walk through it with you. That's my job."

After a deep breath, Mateo said, "I really liked everything we did this weekend. No, that's not true. I *loved* everything we did. But I'm not sure I could have done it with anyone else. Anyone who wasn't Jeff. And I'm worried that after everything we talked about that's not going to be enough for you."

Buckley smiled, seeming unfazed by Mateo's deepest fear. "Those fantasies, the Vegas thing, the bachelor party, those aren't things I really want to do. But you were right. They're all about the same thing. You deciding who to share me with. You making me yours."

"The bachelor party fantasy, though. That was different. That's kinda about betrayal."

"Well, if I asked you to do it, it wouldn't be a betrayal, would it?"

Mateo couldn't help but laugh. He held Buckley's face in his hands as he gazed into his eyes. "For me, there's a big difference between sharing you with Jeff and being inside another man who's not you. I'm not sure I'm all that crazy about the second thing."

Buckley smiled. "So my ass is one of a kind?"

"It is, but be serious, *papi*."

Buckley looked up into his eyes. "If it's not something you want to do, then it stops being a fantasy for me. And I have to say I don't mind being the only man you want to be inside of. But for me, being shared by you is about being owned by you. And that's what I want more than anything."

"And if I don't want to share you with anyone other than Jeff?"

Buckley raised one eyebrow. "You realize you're giving up the opportunity to rail some hot bottom in the middle of our bedroom while I watch?"

"I'd have to be in love with them, and you'd have to be falling for them, too. Because that's what made this weekend work for me. I mean, that is what's happening, right? You're falling for each other. Hard. And I already love you both, so the sight of it, the way you two are with each other, it makes me…thrilled. I don't know how else to describe it."

Buckley's eyes fluttered shut. He shook his head gently. "You don't have to describe it. I can feel it. Last night, when the two of you were…"

That Buckley, who never had trouble using the frankest of sexual terms, had suddenly gone silent while describing one of their sessions, was a sign that he'd been transported by the memory of it.

"It was like I could feel what the two of you feel for each other moving through me. And it was… I thought I was going to die. But, like, a good death. A happy death."

"Don't the Italians call an orgasm the little death?"

Buckley caressed the side of his face. "That's the French, but don't worry. You're cute."

They listened to the surf for a while.

"So if we do this…" Mateo finally started, forcing himself to take another breath before he continued. "You would be okay if it was just the three of us. You, me, and Jeff. And no one else."

"Beyond okay."

"And if he says this was just a one-time thing?"

Buckley lifted his head from Mateo's chest and gazed up at him with a wistful smile. "We'll always have zucchini."

Shaking with laughter, Mateo slapped Buckley lightly on the ass with one hand.

<h1 style="text-align:center">15</h1>

The business center was a glorified closet. When Jeff had first found the place, he'd worried someone might accuse him of hogging the room's single computer. But in the two hours or so since he'd let the glass door drift shut behind him, no one had so much as poked their head in. The age of Docusign and personal devices for toddlers probably spelled doom for hotel business centers in general, and in another year this space would be commandeered by the fitness center next door.

At any rate, he was grateful for his solitude. No prying eyes or curious questions. No need to put a polite spin on what he was working on.

I'm coming up with a battle plan for how to make a throuple work with a guy I've been in love with for years and another guy who makes me feel like I'm flying whenever he touches me.

He changed the font again. From Times New Roman to Optima this time, wondering if a less rounded typeface might make the whole thing feel less like word salad tossed by a fear-addled mind.

Objective 1
Action Items to Define Terms
1. Buckley defines what "poly" means for him.
2. Buckley experiments with Mateo and another third, see if a "closed throuple" is what he wants.
3. Mateo does same.
4. Up to Buckley and Mateo to define whether these experi-

mentation sessions will include the other partner.

5. Buckley and Mateo must complete at least two experimentation sessions before reporting back to Jeff with results of their findings.

6. Three of us to see each other one day a week when Mateo comes down to San Diego for his therapy session.

Results of their findings?

Jesus, what was wrong with him?

He was talking about something that was supposed to be an affair of the heart like it belonged in cargo bays and equipment lockers.

Was it an affair of the heart, though? Or was it little more than the gyrations of three very horny male bodies over the course of a single weekend? That's clearly what all three of them needed to talk about. Instead, here he was in a lightly air-conditioned closet, tapping away on a three-generations-out-of-date Mac.

Maybe phrases like *objectives* and *action items* wouldn't have seemed so cold and inappropriate if he hadn't included about twenty-five mentions of each in a single three-page document. He'd meant to write something focusing, clarifying. Lean and to the point. Instead, what he'd typed up read like a list of a dozen things Buckley and Mateo had to do on their own before Jeff could feel comfortable risking his heart.

The words *closed throuple* stared at him accusingly from the screen. A bright, shining diamond of truth amidst the swirl of anxious proclamations.

He'd come undone last night. For the first time, he'd felt the power and force of a physical connection flowing through three people at once, with equal and shattering force. Like he'd plugged himself into some new power source for the first time and it had rocketed him out of his skin before he'd returned to a body that felt stronger, more powerful, save for one mixed-up head and very confused heart.

He didn't want to be their guest star or the sex toy or their visiting dick.

He wanted them, both of them. He wanted the three of them together, feeding off each other. Feasting on each other. But who was he to ask them to make that kind of commitment?

He was in his mid-forties and they were barely out of their

twenties and discovering their polyamorous sides for the first time. Buckley's big realization that weekend seemed like the beginning of something—for him. Him *and* Mateo.

In the Marines, this level of strategic overthink had always helped him.

In his personal life, it ruined things before they'd begun.

And that's what he felt on the verge of doing now.

Ruining something amazing, unexpected, and wonderful.

He'd put in too much work on the damn thing to delete it, so he added his final summation to the end.

If we pursue this, I want you both to myself.

His hand shook when he clicked the print button.

Halfway across the lobby, a woman called out to him and he spun, having trouble placing the voice.

"I didn't know you stayed the weekend!" Mateo's sister Marisol was walking toward him across the lobby, enfolding him in a big, perfume-scented hug before he could tuck his fresh printout to his chest. "Listen, do you know what room they're in? The front desk won't tell me and neither of them are answering my texts."

"They're in one of the villas. 6E. Why? Is something wrong?"

"Wrong? I don't think so. *Intense*, maybe." She pointed in the direction of the restaurant. A couple who looked a little older than Jeff sat silently at one of the glass tables, heads bowed in deep thought, hands linked across the table. Maybe they were praying. The man had Mateo's height and wavy ink-black hair. The woman had his rounded chin and curious brown eyes. "Are those…"

Marisol nodded. "I'll give you the short version. Father Jones, the prick who tried to destroy our family, got caught stealing from the church *and* sending the money to a girlfriend in Santa Barbara."

Jeff swallowed, looked to Marisol to make sure she wasn't kidding. "Catholic priests aren't allowed to have girlfriends," he finally said.

"Stealing's out too. Mom was so devastated she took to her bed two weeks ago. I didn't want to tell Teo 'cause I didn't want to distract from his party. But the party was tearing her up all weekend. I mean, it's not like I don't understand. She disowned her son on the advice of a thieving hypocrite, and she was too humiliated to ask him to forgive her. But this morning, she finally had enough of feeling sorry for herself. Made me drive them both down here. They want to make things right. And they want to meet Buckley." Her eyes lit up, and she clapped her hands together. "Kind of a great birthday present, right?"

Jeff's heart dropped. The confidence that had propelled him away from that cheap old desktop computer started to wither away inside of him.

"So I guess Christmas is back on the table," he said.

Marisol dabbed at her eyes. "Yeah, I think so. Come on. Take us to their room."

She took his hand and gave it a little tug. Everything inside of him tensed up. His feet turned to concrete blocks.

Christmas, he thought. *Mateo's about to get his family and his favorite holiday back, and it's been hard enough for him to do that with one boyfriend. But two?*

"No. It's..." He pointed in the direction of the hallway leading to the villas. "It's that way. This is a family thing. You guys have your moment."

Marisol nodded, but her smile was flickering and fading as if she could sense his sadness and wasn't sure what to make of it.

He headed for the motor court before she could question him.

Had he left something in the villa? Of course not. He'd never planned to stay. He'd been a guest, that was all.

The best thing to do was leave, fast. This was Mateo's moment. More importantly, it was Buckley's moment to be accepted by Mateo's family. Finally. After months of being made to feel like the guy who'd shattered it to pieces. And here he was, seconds away from asking them both to make a commitment to him? Insane.

This was exactly the reality check he needed. The weekend had been wild and hot and wonderful. Now it was over.

It was time for Mateo and Buckley to be the kind of gay couple his parents might finally accept.

And it was time for Jeff to go home and be a grown-up about all this.

At first, Mateo told himself he was imagining the smell. Sweet and floral and deeply familiar, a constant throughout his childhood and most of his adult life as well—up until a few months ago.

His mother's perfume.

He'd been watching mindless reality television with Buckley, fighting the urge to take off in search of Jeff. They needed to give the man his space, Buckley had told him. Everything had happened so fast it was only natural an A-type like Jeff needed time to pull his thoughts together. They could expect a lecture and an overly detailed battle plan, for sure, but both things would be worth it if he was willing to make the leap. So when Mateo shot up off the sofa at the familiar smell, Buckley said "Babe" in a strained voice that made it sound like he thought Mateo was going back on their agreement.

As soon as he opened the door, Mateo found himself staring into those huge brown eyes that had always been able to make him feel either chastised or commended in an instant. He had those eyes too. His mother's eyes. His mother was here. And she was crying. After a few seconds of stunned silence, she threw her arms around him and exploded with a wrenching sob.

Marisol was next to her, and the story came flying out in rapid-fire Spanish. Father Jones. Stealing. A mistress. Their father stepped in behind their mother, placed a hand on her shoulder, his head bowed the way it had been when he'd once forgotten to set the parking brake on their truck and it had almost rolled into the street, its back left bumper catching on a power pole at the last possible second. He'd never seen his parents so crestfallen and weary, or his mother quite this hysterical. Their hugs and apologies, as incoherent as they were, gave him joy, but their obvious shame made it hard to savor.

Then, once they both caught their breath, they turned to Buckley, who was so stunned by their dramatic entrance, he hadn't moved from where he'd first stood up. His eyes were wide and glistening as Mateo's mother moved to him. Gently, she took both of his hands in hers. Then she kissed him on one cheek and then the other.

"Proverbs 12:5," she said quietly. "The thoughts of the righteous are just, the counsels of the wicked are deceitful."

"Okay," Buckley said softly, then he swallowed, which was what he usually did when he was about to cry.

"My son, he is a righteous man. And I allowed a wicked one to drive him from me."

Mateo's father stepped forward and gave Buckley a quick, hard half hug.

Mateo had his mother's full attention again. "Everything he said to me felt wrong. But I ignored it. I ignored what was in my heart because I thought he was a man of God. But he was dishonest and *weak*. And you have always been strong, Mateo. And I let that bad man rise above you in my heart." Taking Mateo's hands, she looked back over one shoulder at Buckley. "Will you join us for Christmas? Both of you?"

Both of them...

Behind his sister, who was sobbing quietly into one fist, the villa's door stood open to the sun-splashed stairs outside. The space beyond was empty.

Both of them...

An invitation for two at the very moment they were about to become three. An invitation he thought he'd lost forever simply for being himself.

He met Buckley's gaze. His soft, wide-eyed gaze, a look that told him it was his decision to make. Buckley gave him a small nod. It said this decision was his to make.

So Mateo made it.

16

The fact that he'd broken a promise to Mateo didn't even occur to Jeff until he was back in his own kitchen, bracing himself against the fridge with one hand, freshly opened beer bottle in the other. The sense of almost instant loss had turned into a dull ache on the ride home. Now it gained sharp edges. Edges of shame and embarrassment.

He'd looked them both right in the eye and told them he wouldn't leave before their meeting, and he'd done precisely that. Worse, hours had gone by and his phone was dark. No calls, no texts. Of course not. They were probably having a celebratory dinner, crying and embracing, so overwhelmed by the joy of their unexpected family reunion that their memories of the night before and the night before that had become a dull, horny haze.

His memories of the time they'd spent together would never become that, he knew.

He'd brushed up against something unforgettable this weekend. A sense of connection that felt perfectly right, perfectly balanced between three equally strong-willed men. A way to love and be intimate with the man who'd filled his dreams for years, and a new love with a man who challenged him while also taking everything he had to give with a seductive, satisfied smile.

But fate had intervened, just like it had when his parents had vanished. Just like it always did when he lost his head, always with the same message. *You don't get good things when you lose control. Stay the course; stick to the plan.*

Now, he had no choice but to draw comfort from his orderly and immaculate apartment, its little reminders of the life he'd built for himself. Sure, he'd looked forward to the moment Buckley might rib him over his meticulously organized storage room, with its shelves of neatly labeled baskets containing everything from cleaning supplies to car parts. But that moment would never come.

Tomorrow morning, bright and early, he'd be back on base, surrounded by deference and respect and Marines he'd know better than to fall for. Their boyfriends included.

Walking out of Sapphire Cove was the right choice. The lack of text messages on his phone was proof.

He'd finished off a second beer and was halfway through a *Top Gun: Maverick* rewatch when there was a knock on his front door.

It was loud.

And it was angry.

As soon as he saw Mateo and Buckley standing on his front stoop, everything felt suddenly reversed. It was the last few hours since he'd left Sapphire Cove that felt vague and unreal, not the passion-filled days before. Those were suddenly vivid and overpowering once more.

Then Mateo shoved him.

It wasn't hard enough to knock him back more than a step. The surprise of it caught him off guard, not the force.

The man who'd dominated his fantasies and dreams for a year and a half took a step inside without being invited, eyes blazing with an anger Jeff had never seen in them before. "Courage is the mental, moral, and physical strength ingrained in Marines. It carries us through the challenges of combat and aids in overcoming fear. It is the inner strength that enables us to do what is right, to adhere to a higher standard of personal conduct and to make tough decisions under stress and pressure."

Jeff backed up another step, which allowed Buckley to step inside behind his boyfriend and pull the front door shut. They were both dressed as they'd been that morning when he'd left.

And Mateo wasn't done. "Honor guides Marines to exemplify the ultimate in ethical and moral behavior. Never *lie*, never cheat or steal; abide by an uncompromising code of integrity; respect human dignity and respect others. Honor compels Marines to act responsibly, to fulfill our obligations and to hold ourselves and others accountable for every action."

"Yeah, I'm actually still a Marine. I don't need the Core Values read to me."

"You kinda do, actually," Buckley said.

"Because you lied to us," Mateo said.

"And then you ran out of there like a little bitch. And news flash. I'm the only little bitch in this relationship." Buckley held several pieces of paper in his right hand. "Also, you need to be better about deleting your files off shared computers. Just sayin'."

His agenda. Christ. He'd been so nervous about risking his heart he'd just left it there, sitting on the screen. And Buckley had found it because they'd gone looking for him. But the remark did little to defuse the tension. And Jeff was caught between revealing how happy he was that they'd come and defending his decision to jet earlier that day.

"How'd it go with your parents?" Jeff asked.

Mateo folded his arms across his chest. "They're expecting you at Christmas."

His ears were deceiving him. They had to be. Swallowing twice didn't dissolve the lump in his throat. His vision of the two men in front of him went wobbly. He blinked madly.

"Unless you have other plans," Buckley finally said. "And other boyfriends."

"Boyfriends," Jeff whispered.

Buckley rustled the papers in his hands again, a thousand-some-odd words of Jeff's anxious list making. He'd put it right there in black and white. He wanted them both. To himself. Then he'd made a quick getaway. Combined, both facts made him feel less like a man and more like a terrified, lovesick boy being given a chance at something he'd never tasted before.

"I thought it would be too much to ask…" he finally said, but then the words left him.

"Of who?" Buckley said.

"I don't know. All of us. Your parents. I knew I didn't want to do it halfway or casual. And I just… I thought it would be too much. I've always felt like…" The prospect of finishing that sentence hurt his chest.

Buckley was softening. Mateo was still rigid and angry, lips pursed, nostrils flaring.

"Well," Buckley finally said, "a very wise and beautiful man said to me recently that it's hard to walk beside someone if you're always putting everybody else's needs ahead of your own. I guess that applies to two someones as well."

To Mateo, he said, "You really told your parents you're with… two men?"

"This Father Jones thing has them reeling. I've never seen them this humbled. I wasn't going to pass up the opportunity."

Buckley whispered, "I kinda thought he should ask for a check, too, but it wasn't my decision."

"How'd you put it?" Jeff asked. "I mean, how did you describe me?"

"I told them I was in love with two men and so was Buckley, and all three of us would be there at the holidays or none of us would be."

Jeff shook his head in disbelief. His voice was a croak. "You said that even after you knew I'd left?"

"I said it *because* you'd left. And I knew why."

"Because I didn't want to get in the way," Jeff whispered.

"Close, but not quite."

Still getting used to this confidence out of his former junior Marine, Jeff studied the man a few feet away.

"Your uncle, the day it was clear your parents weren't coming back, that shitty thing he said to you and your sister…"

For an instant, it was like he was standing in the headlight of an oncoming train. A few deep breaths brought warmth to his limbs, to his extremities, and the headlight turned into a glow that haloed all three of them. He'd told Mateo plenty about his background over the years. The younger man had listened, nodding, but had rarely said anything in response, as if he thought it wasn't his space to offer his thoughts on the older man's difficult past. But he'd been listening to him. He'd been learning about him. He'd been loving him.

"He blamed you for breaking up your family 'cause he couldn't face that your parents were both addicts. Ever since, you've made it your job to keep things together. I mean, Christ, you used to pop wood every time you used the words *unit cohesion*. But this thing, this amazing, beautiful thing, what the three of us did this weekend, you can't keep that together by walking away."

Suddenly Jeff was having trouble standing. Mateo and Buckley had risked being reunited with Mateo's family for him. For the three of them. For what they'd started this weekend.

Outside of a combat situation, he couldn't remember the last time someone had gone to bat for him like this, put it all on the line when the stakes were this high. "I lied to you. I'm sorry. I said I wouldn't walk out and then…I walked out."

"That's not all you did." Buckley's sharp-edged accusation was softened by the fact that he was curving an arm gently around Jeff's lower back.

"And you better never do it again." Mateo's nose was inches from his, his breath tickling Jeff's lips. "Don't ever take away another chance for us to love you."

His eyes drifted shut as Mateo's lips met his. Then they were guiding him into the bedroom. They undressed him gently, unhurriedly, and when the three of them sank down to the comforter together he felt like his bones might meld with the mattress. He felt as if his body were coming to a kind of rest it had never known. Deluding himself into believing fear was actually good sense required a lot of energy, and when it left his body, it seemed to take every ounce of tension with it, a swift departure that made clear how punishing the effort had been to his muscles, his skin, his beating heart.

He gave himself to them, to their stroking hands and their searching, hungry mouths. To their tenacity and their courage and their belief that their wild weekend could become everything he hoped it could be. He felt like a cross between a fallen warrior whose wounds were being expertly tended to and a bitter old man infused with the confidence and spirit of youth. He wanted to cry with relief, with joy, but he kept his tears at bay until later that night.

He was giving them a little tour of his place. When Buckley saw his meticulously organized storage room, his jaw fell open and his blue eyes widened. "Babe, I think we should come clean and admit we're only using Jeff for his ten thousand micro screws arranged by thread diameter."

He managed to wipe away the tear before either man saw it.

Such a tiny, fleeting moment, but it did him in. A few hours earlier he'd been mourning the fact that Buckley might never rib him about his storage room, and here they were. A small miracle that reminded him of the much bigger one that had just changed his life for the better.

17

During the three months he and Mateo spent officially dating their new boyfriend, Buckley had been delighted to learn that he and Jeff had far more in common than their love for the man who'd brought them together. For one, they were equally superstitious.

Jeff always wore the exact same Luis Arráez jersey whenever the three of them went to a Padres game, and on busy holiday weekends, when the calls his ambulance crews received were usually more extreme thanks to hard partying and fireworks, Buckley always donned the same sterling-silver wheat chain necklace, his first, of what he hoped would be many, birthday gifts from Mateo.

Buckley figured this was why he and Jeff had worn nearly matching outfits every time they showed up to support Mateo during one of his test rides in the elevator at his therapist's office building. A long-sleeved collared shirt and blue jeans with dress shoes.

"You guys here to keep me from throwing up or to sell me some real estate?" Mateo had asked the first time they'd all gathered in the building's glossy lobby. It turned out he usually attended his sessions in shorts and a T-shirt, depending on the weather.

Dr. Pete saw his patients in a glass-and-steel office building not far from San Diego International Airport and the Marine Corps Recruit Depot. It was six stories tall, which meant its elevators rose to a height three stories above the longest elevator ride Mateo had endured on his own since starting treatment for his PTSD. On that first day, Dr. Pete had reserved them an elevator with building management, and, clutching Buckley's hand in his right and Jeff's hand in his left, Mateo had made it all the way to the top without asking them to stop at one of the floors in between.

Because it had been such a success, Buckley and Jeff had dressed pretty much the same for every visit since.

Now, four months after their life-changing weekend at Sapphire Cove and one month after they'd officially become a throuple, it was time for Mateo to try the ride alone.

"You sure you guys don't want to head up to the top floor now and wait for me there?" Mateo said as he eyed the elevator doors.

"No worries. We're in pretty good shape." Jeff winked at him.

Mateo raised one eyebrow and gave them both an arch look, clearly doubting their belief that they could race up six flights of stairs in enough time to beat his elevator. Taking one of the unreserved cars meant they might get stopped before they reached the top.

Buckley sensed a different tension right under the surface.

If he and Jeff raced Mateo to the top, that assumed Mateo would make it there himself. If Mateo didn't, would it be less stressful for him to know his boyfriends were waiting for him down in the lobby or at the destination he'd failed to reach on his own?

These thoughts buzzed in Buckley's brain, but he didn't give voice to them. In their support sessions, he was learning to step back and allow Mateo his process. Jeff was too. Both men wanted to come up with the magical to-do list that would make Mateo's fears vanish like smoke. Dr. Pete had convinced them no such list existed, and if it did, Mateo had to be its sole author. Another perk of their throuple was that Buckley and Jeff could share their frustrations over this medical guidance with each other, rather than drowning Mateo with them as he tried to find his own way forward.

A silence fell, interrupted by a gaggle of scrubs-clad nurses returning from lunch who gave them curious looks as they waited for one of the other elevators.

Dr. Pete stepped forward. "Want to run through our coping strategies?"

Mateo nodded. "Box breathing."

Buckley watched the two men like a hawk. He was getting glimpses into an important process he'd been asked to step back from when Mateo started treatment.

Dr. Pete nodded. "Four counts in through the nose, hold four, out through the mouth four. And if you're not feeling it, expand the count from four to six."

When he nodded again, the tense set to Mateo's mouth made Buckley want to reach out and take his hand. He didn't. In moments like this, he needed to trust the process. When Jeff tightened his grip on Buckley's hand, it was clear he was fighting the same urge.

"Time, date, feet," Mateo said.

Dr. Pete nodded. "Ground yourself in the moment you're actually in by repeating the time, the calendar date, and telling yourself exactly where your feet are in the present moment. Get super specific if you need to. City, street, building address, elevator floor, cheap shitty carpet, that kind of thing. Whatever gets you back here, today. In the moment you're actually in."

And not in that goddamn Osprey, Buckley thought.

"And last but not least…"

Mateo answered by holding up his right wrist. A snap with the rubber band wasn't meant to cause pain. But a short, jarring stimulus could often disrupt an anxiety-fueled flight from reality, jolting you back inside your skin.

Mateo sucked in a deep breath.

"And we'll be waiting for you at the top," Jeff offered.

"To suck your dick." Suddenly everyone was looking at Buckley and that's when he realized he'd said those words out loud.

Fighting laughter, Jeff slapped him on the ass. Smiling, Mateo shook his head at his boyfriend—the loudest and most inappropriate one. At least he'd cut the tension.

"Sorry, doc," Buckley added.

"Let's hold off on the celebratory intimacy until we're home. I don't want to lose my lease here."

Buckley nodded. Jeff furtively squeezed his ass cheek.

Mateo sucked in a deep breath and turned to both men. They wrapped their arms around him in a tight, three-way hug. Then, eyes averted, as if summoning his courage, Mateo slapped them both on the back. "Get cracking or I'll beat you there."

Buckley and Jeff raced to the nearest fire stairway door.

The next thing he knew they were flying up the concrete stairs. They'd scoped out the route earlier and propped the door open on the sixth floor. Buckley was grateful for the exertion. It distracted him from imagining the disappointed look on Mateo's face if he had to pull the rip cord before making the complete trip.

Then, before he knew it, they exploded, gasping, into the carpeted elevator lobby on the sixth floor. There was Mateo, arms folded across his chest.

"You boys need to do more cardio."

This time their three-way hug was tighter. And that was a good thing because Buckley was crying a little, and this gave him an excuse to bury his face in Mateo's T-shirt.

Per the doctor's orders, they returned home before engaging in celebratory intimacy. But they didn't make it any farther than the kitchen.

Christmas shopping started the next day.

Not the kind where you bought gifts for your loved ones, but the kind where Mateo bought out every World Market within a hundred-mile radius for the props he needed to transform his parents' living room into a glittering winter wonderland. And their living room as well. He'd visited the family home in Huntington Park several times to do so-called planning sessions for their decorations, but Buckley knew these were re-entry meetings, chances for Mateo to get comfortable with his parents again on his own before the gathering that would bring them all together at the holidays.

Typically, he'd head out the door with one instruction for the men he loved. "Be sure to fuck each other's brains out while I'm gone so you've got plenty of details to share with me when I'm back."

This was one of the many boundaries they'd negotiated the night of Jeff's now infamous walkout at Sapphire Cove.

Buckley had been reluctant to agree to Jeff's proposal of a three-month dating period before the three of them dove in balls first. But Mateo had convinced him and so they'd confined their time with Jeff to sleepovers at his place once a week when Mateo needed to be in San Diego for therapy.

When they weren't having blazing sex, they talked through all the boundaries and rules needed to make their unconventional situation work.

Other people were off the table.

As for how many of them were required to make a quorum, Mateo, it seemed, was completely addicted to the thrills he got from Buckley and Jeff going at it while he was out of the house. One of his kinks, it turned out, was something he called *cuck adjacent*, without the humiliation role-play that went along with that seemingly more popular role-play fantasy. When he had to be someplace he couldn't leave quickly without consequences—usually a class at school—Jeff would start texting him about the filthy things he was doing to Buckley while he was gone. Sometimes with a dirty picture or two thrown in. To hear him tell it, the texts were sweet torture, a form of edging more intense than any he'd ever known, and by the time he returned home he was practically bursting out of his jeans. During sessions like this, he'd fuck the breath out of Buckley and sometimes fuck Jeff's mouth so hard, tears would sprout from the older man's eyes.

Jeff, for his part, preferred sweeter photos of the two of them whenever he was away.

If the men he loved lying on top of each other with their bare asses stacked like cakes and aimed at the camera could be called sweet.

To Buckley's very delighted surprise, it also turned out Jeff enjoyed being tied up and worked over, something he'd always been afraid to admit to with his partners because he had no desire to engage in the bottoming that most folks rashly assumed went hand in hand with submission. There were other ways to submit to a man without letting him fuck your ass, and Jeff had apparently discovered all of them, with a very special toy box and some coils of friction-free rope.

Once those first three months were over, Jeff started driving north to their place on a regular basis. It was clear to Buckley he hadn't wanted to feel like an outsider or a third wheel in their bedroom before they were all sure the foundation they were building was solid.

Two months after Mateo's victorious elevator ride to the top floor of his therapist's office building, Christmas Eve was spent at the Cano family home in Huntington Park. The house was packed, and even though most of his family was careful to avoid the subject, Mateo's relatives seemed energized by his return.

The three of them even held hands as they walked the last of the Posadas, a Christmas tradition neither Buckley nor Jeff had ever experienced before that night. Led by the angel-costumed, six-year-old daughter of Mateo's cousin, the entire family formed a procession to a neighbor's house, many of them carrying statues of shepherds and small angels. When they arrived at their destination, they were ceremonially denied entrance, as Joseph and Mary were denied entrance to the inn, but given refreshments as compensation. Then they filed outside to the yard where Jeff did an excellent job of watching over the kids as they smashed the tar out of a piñata and—largely thanks to Jeff—not each other.

Then it was back to the Cano home for gift giving, where every now and then Gracie Cano would pause whatever she was doing and reach out and grasp her son's hand, closing her eyes briefly, perhaps to avoid shedding tears, as if her son had been returned to her after a long imprisonment.

Buckley had never seen Mateo interact with his family for such an extended period, and it warmed his heart to see his boyfriend give every new arrival a tour of the decorations he'd assembled throughout the house, the ones that weren't playing music or sound effects that drowned out his explanations. This was a sweet, innocent and joyful side of Mateo that made Buckley fall in love with him all over again. Then came the gifts. Once it became clear that almost all the relatives in attendance had brought something for both Buckley and Jeff, Buckley glanced over at Jeff to see if he was tearing up too, and the man gruffly muttered, "Stay focused on the unwrapping here. We've got a lot to get through." A stern command that made clear their master sergeant was on the verge of a good cry as well.

It was probably the first and last time the two of them would ever cry over a pair of socks made to look like reindeer heads, but that was beside the point.

Christmas morning was theirs to celebrate at home.

The display under the tree at their townhouse was no less impressive than the one Mateo had assembled for his parents.

Only this one would play host to a very special celebration for just the three of them.

18

Dressed in his best version of a slutty elf costume, Buckley padded barefoot into the living room. His bright red shorts matched his cap. They also barely covered his thighs. He was freshly showered and shirtless under his fuzzy green vest. He'd drawn the line at goofy shoes.

When he entered the winter wonderland in their living room there was not one, but two, muscular Santas waiting for him on the sofa, affecting their best disciplinary scowls under their silly white beards.

"Ho, ho, ho," Jeff growled, with nothing that sounded like Christmas cheer.

"Looks like someone forgot to leave out the milk and cookies." Mateo stood.

Don't laugh, Buckley told himself.

"I didn't realize you worked in pairs, Santa."

Maybe his comment betrayed the fact he thought the whole thing was kind of silly, but a little snarky defiance from their bottom usually amped Jeff and Mateo up a notch, no matter the fantasy.

Both his boyfriends were advancing on him now. "Only when we have to deal with the naughtiest elves."

Mateo slapped his ass. Buckley tried to focus on the man's beautiful brown chest, visible through the top few undone buttons of his costume, and not the incredibly stupid beard. *Buckley Has Two Santas* had been Jeff's fantasy of choice, not his. But he'd learned it was important to stay open and inclusive when it came to three-way role-play. When he'd first pitched it to them, neither man had been especially wild about his kidnapping fantasy, but they'd done everything they could to make it work safely. Jeff had even drilled extra—and in Buckley's view, unnecessary—holes in the trunk of the car to be sure Buckley could breathe during the ride to the dingy motel they'd picked out for Buckley's mock violation.

"The ones who make Santa hungry," Jeff growled.

Jeff slapped his ass.

I can definitely make this work, Buckley thought as the two gruff, growling Santas pushed his vest off his body.

Then they pushed him to his knees.

The sight of them fishing their impressive cocks out of their red-and-white pants ignited a naughty thrill in him that burned off his last misgivings about the scene. Their beards and Santa caps, which had seemed so silly a second before, worked the same exhilarating power on him as the stocking caps he'd made them wear during his mock abduction a few weeks before. As if he'd been turned into a vessel for pure pleasure by two men driven to the far edge of their shame by their uncontrollable desire for him.

His two Santas started out rough and aggressive, spearing his mouth in turn to show him who was boss, but soon, his skillful cock sucking overpowered them and both men stood rigid and helpless whenever he devoted his full attention to them. Over the past few months, he'd studied the different maps of pleasure along their shafts like they were maps charting the road home after a long exile in the desert. The top of Mateo's head was his most sensitive part and when Buckley swirled his tongue back and forth over it, the moans the man made sounded like pleas.

Jeff's most sensitive spot was where his shaft met his balls and when Buckley flickered his tongue across that special space, he'd always grit his teeth and grip the back of Buckley's head in a way that melted Buckley's spine. "Dirty little elf," the older man growled now. "Dirty, slutty little elf."

Buckley pulled back as much as he could against the power of Jeff's grip, enough so that he could stare up at the man with his best puppy-dog eyes. "Are my Santas still hungry?"

Jeff's grin was big enough to see through his fake beard. "Yeah, but who gives a damn about cookies when there's cake."

In an instant, they'd jerked him to his feet, and suddenly he was being led into the middle of the living room. Then he was down on all fours as a seated Jeff fed his cock back into his mouth. From behind, Mateo pulled Buckley's shorts down, exposing his ass to the air before lavishing it in the wet warmth of his flickering tongue. He'd doffed the beard, another reminder this scene was building to something special—something that still felt new, that still required all their patience and practice. And Mateo's excitement was obvious from the wide, hungry, lapping strokes he was giving Buckley's hole and crack. This was new, this wild oral ravishment he was giving Buckley's entire ass, fueled no doubt by his knowledge that he was about to share it with Jeff.

Once he could bring himself to pull his mouth from Jeff's cock, Buckley managed a breathless query. "Did you bring me any toys, Santas?"

"Sure we did, little elf," Mateo said into his cheeks, "but did you earn them, though?"

"Oh yeah," Jeff said, then punctuated it with a light slap of his hard cock across Buckley's spit-soaked right cheek. "He's earned them. He's earned them good and dirty."

Buckley closed his eyes, listening intently as Mateo tore open one of the wrapped presents under the tree behind him. The contents wouldn't be a surprise, but an essential tool to prepare him for what was to come. As always, Mateo wielded it expertly. After dousing it with lube from the same pre-placed gift box, he worked the wide butt plug up into Buckley with slow, steady skill, waiting for him to open around it, tenderly rubbing his other hand across his lower back to encourage his resistance to fade.

Once the first shockwaves of entry finished shuddering through him, Buckley reached forward and gently tugged the curly white beard off Jeff's face. His boyfriend didn't fight him. Role-play was fun, but if they were both going to take him at once, he needed them to stop being Santas and go back to being the men who'd changed his life.

The cap could stay, though. There was something sexy about the playful counterpoint it made to the blazing intensity in Jeff's expression.

"Are you ready, baby?" Mateo whispered in his ear, still working the plug into him with one hand. "Are you ready to be ours?"

He'd read Buckley's body and the depth of his silence and dropped the Santa routine.

Buckley nodded.

Their movements became slow, languid, careful. Gently, Mateo extracted the butt plug. Embracing him front and back, both men straightened Buckley until he was sitting on his haunches. In the moments before a dual claiming, Buckley needed to be kissed, held, made to feel safe. The first time they'd managed to slide inside of him at once had been an experience marked by equal parts terror and joy, a second loss of virginity, something deep and special he'd given only to the men he now shared a life with.

They gently unfolded Buckley's legs as Mateo lay down on the floor under him.

Because he now had the greatest freedom of movement, Jeff took control, finding the lube bottle, slathering it across his cock and then Mateo's and then Buckley's.

Jeff's fingers entered him first, and he gazed into his eyes as he explored. Reading him for any resistance or fear. Whenever he saw it, he usually chased it away with comforting words. But right now, he saw none because Buckley felt none.

To be taken like this made Buckley feel utterly seen.

Jeff guided Mateo's cock inside of Buckley slowly, swallowing one of Buckley's startled moans with a hungry kiss. Then it was time for Jeff to add his own. Slowly, persistently, face pressed to Buckley's, their noses touching.

They'd arrived at the moment of truth. The moment when Buckley's body would either surrender or rebel. They'd managed it four times out of six. Buckley felt his thighs tingle now, a good sign. Jeff could feel it too.

Then Jeff's bare, slick shaft joined Mateo's, and Buckley closed his eyes and saw welcome stars.

Both men had deliciously different reactions whenever Buckley yielded to them at once.

Mateo went into a kind of awestruck trance, breathing deeply against Buckley's neck, kissing the nape gently, holding him as tightly as he could.

Jeff's jaw would tense and his eyes would blaze wildly, as if the feel of Mateo's shaft rubbing along his inside Buckley's hole was sending electric currents coursing through him. The first time Jeff's reactions had frightened Buckley because he'd thought these were signs the man might start plowing away at him with too much force.

But his fears had been for naught.

It was time to rock and grind. Slow and steady, but wonderfully rhythmic, determined. And the miracle of it, as they'd all agreed after the first time, was that all three men felt like they were getting fucked. Connected and consumed by that same force that had claimed them the first time Jeff had filled Buckley at Sapphire Cove.

When Buckley's eyes opened now, they flitted over the picture of Jeff and Mateo hanging on their living room wall, the one that had given birth to a secret fantasy turned blissful reality. He erupted. Hands free at first until Jeff saw the first slick of his seed, seized his lube-slick cock and stroked. Buckley released a primal wail. Jeff let out the low series of *oh's*. He was close.

After their first weekend together, Jeff had confessed how turned on he'd been watching Mateo finish in Buckley's mouth, and so, almost every time they'd had sex since becoming exclusive, Buckley had given his new boyfriend what they hadn't felt safe to do at Sapphire Cove. Or, more accurately, he let Jeff give it to him.

Withdrawing from Buckley, Jeff sank back onto his haunches. Carefully, without pulling himself free, Mateo scooted back, letting Buckley lean forward onto his knees. Doggy style, and now alone inside him, Mateo quickened his thrusts as Buckley opened his mouth inches away from Jeff's stroking hand. Whatever expression was on Buckley's face, it brought a glazed-eyed look of wonderment to Jeff's. Buckley parted his lips, tried to keep his eyes wide and fixed on Jeff's. But Mateo's expert, unleashed fucking was making him dizzy with bliss and it was hard to keep his eyes open.

Then Jeff erupted with a bellow.

Buckley felt anointed, blessed. Fed.

At the sight of his other boyfriend painting Buckley's face, Mateo exploded, filling Buckley with deep, punching jabs.

For what felt like an eternity, each man struggled to catch his breath.

"How are we going to top that for New Year's?" Buckley asked.

Laughing, they fell into a tangle on the floor, their costumes either mostly discarded or barely clinging to their sweaty bodies. Mateo had ended up in the middle. Buckley hooked one leg over his and rested his head on his chest, reaching down to gently stroke his deflating cock. He looked up, saw Jeff and Mateo kissing with such passion and force he felt his own cock jerk.

A shower and one hearty breakfast later, it was time for a more civilized gift exchange.

Buckley and Mateo saved their special gift for Jeff until the end. When he opened the box and removed a small shiny new key, he looked confused by its small size. He already had a key to their apartment, even though he hadn't moved in. "What's this to?" Jeff finally asked.

"A new storage locker," Buckley answered. "About ten minutes from here."

"I've got plenty of room in my storage room."

"Yeah," Mateo said, scooting across the sea of wrapping paper so he could slide an arm around Jeff's back, "but it's an hour away."

Buckley said, "That way you won't have to drive an hour south when you need your special wrench set because mine is apparently"—Buckley mimed air quotes—"*not fit to tighten the screws on a toy train.*"

Looking back and forth between the two of them, nostrils flaring from deep breaths he was trying to restrain. "You boys expecting me to do some work around the house?"

"Maybe," Buckley said softly, looking up at him. "Once it's yours."

"Once you move in," Mateo added.

Jeff smiled.

Was the man tearing up a little? He had a tendency to do that, mostly when he thought Buckley and Jeff weren't looking, in moments when he seemed happier than he'd ever been before.

Their mouths met, one after the other, and then in a sequence more random and frenzied.

"Fine," Jeff said, "but we're going to need a bigger bed."

Buckley smiled. "As long as I can sleep in the middle."

Jeff slapped his ass. "Who said anything about sleeping?"

But they did sleep that night, all three of them, and peacefully, knowing they'd passed another milestone in the journey that had begun during one wild weekend at a place called Sapphire Cove. A journey none of them wanted to end.

Connor and Logan After Dark

I've reached the end of everything Buckley shared with me earlier that night. A silence falls as I caress my husband's thickening cock underneath the sheet.

"Sweet story," Logan finally says, but the raw edge in his voice betrays the arousal I can feel in my grip.

Maybe it's just my hand that's doing it, or maybe he's as turned on as I am by the tale I just told.

Or maybe it was how I told the tale that got him hot. Like it was some naughty piece of smut I downloaded off the internet purely for our pleasure. What I've really done is push us further and further away from what disturbed me about Buckley's call to begin with, and I'm not sure how long we can hover in this space before the real reason for my sleeplessness intrudes again.

"So why did it freak you out?" Logan asks.

And there it is, *I think. One of the great things about our marriage is that it's almost impossible for me to deflect. He always gently zeroes in on the source of my discomfort. Even if I sometimes find myself singing and tap dancing to have the same effect on him.*

I look at him through the shadows of our bedroom. The sheet's fallen away from his torso, exposing his tan, tree-trunk-thick thighs.

"I'm worried," is all I manage. As he waits for me to finish, he reaches out through the dark and caresses the side of my face. His brow is gently furrowed.

"About what, my prince?"

I'm never going to speak my truth if I don't stop playing with my husband's magnificent cock. We have, quite often throughout our relationship and marriage, used sex to avoid difficult topics. He used it when it came to discussions of our wedding, the planning of which raised complicated feelings for him that delayed everything until they were addressed.

Slowly, I lift myself into a seated position and lean back against the mountain of pillows, taking one of his hands in mine and holding it to my chest. I clutch it tightly, as if the conversation we're about to have might tear me from him like a twister's winds.

"I've never said anything to make you feel like I want a three-way, have I?" Logan finally says. "'Cause that's really not something I want."

"No, but...some of Buckley's fantasies. The things he talked about feeling about Mateo...I feel them about you. Like, I think about you with you other guys. A lot."

"Like in a freaked-out way or in a—"

"Like in a jerking off at home when you're visiting Donnie down in San Diego kind of way."

My husband is clearly trying not to laugh as he curves his free arm across my shoulders. "I see."

"Do you, though? 'Cause I'm not sure I do. Does it mean I'm polyamorous too?"

"Tell me something, these guys you imagine me with. Are they real people?"

"You mean, like, are they werewolves?"

Logan laughs. "Are they people we actually know?"

"No, they're mostly faceless twinks."

"Faceless twinks. So, like, ghost twinks?"

"Babe. Be serious."

Logan clears his throat and tightens the half embrace he has me in until my head is sinking to his chest. "Okay. Serious, then. I think some of this is about the whole Sergeant Stud thing. I know my manwhore past can be challenging sometimes—"

"It's not, babe. I promise. I—"

"I know. Just hold on a second. I'm saying, I think there might still be a part of you that worries I gave all those boys something I didn't give you. And so you want to see it. In your mind's eye, or whatever. So you can demystify it. Or feel like you were part of it. But trust me, Connor, the opposite is true. I mean, most of the time, I *wouldn't even kiss those tricks. It was just like scratching an itch or getting a burst of validation.*

"But the other thing is this, and this is important. Fantasies are just fantasies, babe. A fantasy can never be wrong. Only actions can be wrong. And besides, I have plenty of fantasies about you and other guys. The other night when you had to work late, I got off to the thought of the entire security department running a train on you in your office."

I lift my head from his chest in surprise. "Jesus, really? That's intense."

"Well, it's not happening so you don't need to worry about the intensity level, okay?" The protective edge in his voice thrills me.

I stroke his chest to calm him, but I'm relieved to hear his dirty thoughts about me when I'm not around run the same taboo gamut mine do, so relieved that I no longer care we're both going to be hurting for sleep tomorrow.

Logan takes a deep breath. "What I'm saying here is, the story you told isn't about fantasies. It's about three men who all fell in love with each other. And if, God forbid, the day comes where you and I ever fall in love with the same person, we can talk about it. But I don't know how soon we're going to get there 'cause I usually threaten the life of anyone who looks at your ass for longer than ten seconds."

"That's really hot, babe. The possessiveness thing." I meet his lips through the shadows, and the flicker of his tongue against mine sends white-hot heat racing up my spine. "It's really, really hot."

"Another sign we're not cut out for throuple life," Logan whispers. "You wanting me to rip the arms off anyone who tries to make a move on you and all. Doesn't sound very polyamorous to me."

I laugh, feeling a relief in it I haven't felt for hours.

Logan studies me. "We didn't grow up with a lot of gay role models, you and me. Not when it came to relationships anyway. So sometimes it can feel like we have to do everything our friends are doing. But we don't. Buckley and Mateo and Jeff...their story's their story. And our story is ours. And they're both beautiful stories. There's nothing wrong with them. Or with us."

The tension that's been with me since I got off the phone finally leaves me as I wilt into his embrace.

"There was one thing about their story I really did like,

though...” Logan finally says. I sit up again. He raises one eyebrow and gives me a half-cocked grin. “The whole role-play thing. We could stand to do a lot more work on that front.”

“Oh yeah?”

He turns to me, reaching for both my wrists, and before I know it he’s pinning me to our bed, his weight, strength and size combining in a gentle wave that pushes me into the submission I crave. His nose is inches from mine and he’s gently grinding his massive cock against my super-sensitive hole in the way he knows will drive me wild.

“Yeah,” he growls, before planting a long, leisurely kiss on my lips. “I’ve got a lot of ideas.”

“So do I,” I manage when we break for air.

“Like?” Logan asks.

“Like you’re a masked intruder who breaks into the house while I’m home alone and forces me to service you on my knees. Or you’re a difficult guest and when I go to your suite to ask how I can make it right, you bend me over the bed and force me to give you the customer service you really crave. Or it’s my first day working as a cabana boy at the hotel and you give me a security briefing. In your office. With your cock.”

“Wow. You were very *ready for this conversation.”*

“Fantasies can never be wrong, right?”

His kiss is forceful and hungry. “Not with you, they can’t,” he says when he finally comes up for air.

A few minutes later, freed of my guilt and my shame, I am riding him, and it feels like we’re joined by more than our bodies and our hearts, but by our filthy minds as well. Dirty imaginations we’ve now pledged to share the same way we share our lives and our home and souls.

Released of these burdens and filled by the man who makes me whole, I am free once again to be proud of the place we built, the place we saved, the place that has satisfied the cravings and the hearts of so many men like us.

THE END

Acknowledgments from the Author

I am grateful to the Blue Box Press team for giving this novella the same love and support they've given to my novels in the Sapphire Cove series. Co-owners Liz Berry and Jillian Stein, and amazing editors Kim Guidroz and Stacey Tardiff, thanks for all that you've done for this spicy little story.

Thanks to Imogen Howson for a wonderful edit and proofread. As my best friend, and co-owner of our production company Dinner Partners, *New York Times* bestselling author Eric Shaw Quinn likes to say whenever Immi edits one of his wonderful books. "Please don't hire her. She's all ours." (Just kidding. Sort of.)

For ensuring the accurate portrayal of Marine Corps terminology and operations, profound gratitude goes to Lieutenant Colonel M. Matthew Phelps, USMC. Any mistakes made in these areas are those of the author.

Shortly before this novella was finished, the Blue Box family suffered an incalculable loss with the untimely and sudden passing of M.J. Rose, one of the company's founders and a perpetual champion of my romance writing. During the last meal we shared together, she told me they'd be happy to publish this story. It's a memory I will treasure always. There would be no Sapphire Cove without M.J. Her witty and sophisticated memory will love on in its lavish suites and spacious balconies and many other nooks and alcoves where she encouraged its many stories to grow.

Discover More Christopher Rice

Sapphire Sunset
Sapphire Cove, Book 1
By Christopher Rice writing as C. Travis Rice

For the first time *New York Times* bestselling author Christopher Rice writes as C. Travis Rice. Under his new pen name, Rice offers tales of passion, intrigue, and steamy romance between men. The first novel, SAPPHIRE SUNSET, transports you to a beautiful luxury resort on the sparkling Southern California coast where strong-willed heroes release the shame that blocks their heart's desires.

Logan Murdoch is a fighter, a survivor, and a provider. When he leaves a distinguished career in the Marine Corps to work security at a luxury beachfront resort, he's got one objective: pay his father's mounting medical bills. That means Connor Harcourt, the irresistibly handsome scion of the wealthy family that owns Sapphire Cove, is strictly off-limits, despite his sassy swagger and beautiful blue eyes. Logan's life is all about sacrifices; Connor is privilege personified. But temptation is a beast that demands to be fed, and a furtive kiss ignites instant passion, forcing Logan to slam the brakes. Hard.

Haunted by their frustrated attraction, the two men find themselves hurled back together when a headline-making scandal threatens to ruin the resort they both love. This time, there's no easy escape from the magnetic pull of their white hot desire. Will saving Sapphire Cove help forge the union they crave, or will it drive them apart once more?

Sapphire Spring
Sapphire Cove, Book 2
By Christopher Rice writing as C. Travis Rice

Naser Kazemi has never met a problem a good spending plan couldn't fix. But working as the chief accountant for his best friend's resort isn't turning out to be the dream job he'd hoped for. It doesn't help that his fashion designer sister is planning an event that just might bring Sapphire Cove crashing down all around them. When the wild party unexpectedly reunites him with Mason Worther, the gorgeous former jock who made his high school experience a living hell, things go from bad to seductive.

The former golden boy's adult life is a mess, and he knows it's time to reform his hard partying ways. But for Mason, cleaning up his act means cleaning up his prior misdeeds. And he plans to start with Naser, by submitting to whatever the man demands of him to make things right. The offer ignites an all-consuming passion both men have denied for years. But can they confront their painful past without losing each other in the process?

Sapphire Storm
Sapphire Cove, Book 3
By Christopher Rice writing as C. Travis Rice

Ethan Blake has dedicated his life to satisfying other people's appetites. At forty-three, he's finally landed his dream job—head pastry chef at an exclusive resort. Now he's got a jet-setting career that's taken him to romantic locations all over the world. But years before, after his parents threw him out for being gay, Ethan supported himself in a manner he'd rather keep under the covers today.

Roman Walker is a twenty-five-year-old fitness celebrity awash in thirsty followers. But when he walks through the doors of Sapphire Cove, it's not just to oversee the menu for his celebrity client's wedding. Decades ago, Roman and Ethan crossed paths on a New York street corner during a terrible, life-changing moment that scarred them both. Now Roman's back for revenge.

But when his plan goes wildly off the rails, Roman suddenly finds himself at the center of an even stranger and darker plot concocted by his most famous client. Well-versed in the ways of the wealthy and the entitled, Roman's former target offers to be his strongest ally during a moment that might derail the young man's newfound career. But the experienced older man's offer also ignites an irresistible and forbidden attraction that threatens to consume them both, even as it exposes old secrets and incurs the wrath of the powerful and the famous.

Sapphire Dawn
Sapphire Cove, Book 4
By Christopher Rice writing as C. Travis Rice

Donnie Bascombe has made a lot of people's fantasies come true in his life, first in the bedroom, then on the set of his adult entertainment studio. To escape his difficult background, he made sex his business. But his best friend Logan Murdoch has just presented him with his tallest order yet — help plan the wedding of his dreams to wealthy hotelier Connor Harcourt. Desire has always been Donnie's forte. But lavish nuptials at one of Southern California's premier oceanfront resorts? For that job, he'll need a partner. And a mentor. Preferably someone who can put up with the fact that his idea of elegant is a buffet with a salad bar.

Richard Merriweather has devoted his life to planning fairy tale weddings for celebrities and royalty — only to have his own husband shatter his heart into a million pieces. Remaking the special events office at Sapphire Cove is just the distraction he needs to get his fancy and luxurious life back on track. But turning the wedding between the resort's general manager and security director into the most stunning and talked about in its history will require him to work alongside the groom's brash and undeniably sexy best friend. Worse, Donnie Bascombe has a powerful attraction to Richard Merriweather he can't keep secret.

If Richard can show Donnie how to make his best friends happy, Donnie promises to behave himself. But the more Richard gets to know the sweet, affectionate hormone ball, the less he wants him to behave. And that's a problem. Because Richard Merriweather doesn't do hook ups and Donnie doesn't do relationships. Or does he? The closer Donnie gets to Richard, the more he wants something different, something he's never had before. Something more. Something that will force both men to confront the heartbreak in their pasts as they plan Sapphire Cove's wedding of the decade and find an unexpected future for themselves.

Dance of Desire
By Christopher Rice

When Amber Watson walks in on her husband in the throes of extramarital passion with one of his employees, her comfortable, passion-free life is shattered in an instant. Worse, the fate of the successful country music bar that bears her family's name suddenly hangs in the balance. Her soon to be ex-husband is one of the bar's official owners; his mistress, one of its employees. Will her divorce destroy her late father's legacy?

Not if Amber's adopted brother Caleb has anything to do with it. The wandering cowboy has picked the perfect time for a homecoming. Better yet, he's determined to use his brains and his fists to put Amber's ex in his place and keep the family business intact. But Caleb's long absence has done nothing to dim the forbidden desire between him and the woman the State of Texas considers to be his sister.

Years ago, when they were just teenagers, Caleb and Amber shared a passionate first kiss beside a moonlit lake. But that same night, tragedy claimed the life of Caleb's parents and the handsome young man went from being a family friend to Amber's adopted brother. Has enough time passed for the two of them to throw off the roles Amber's father picked for them all those years ago? Will their desire for each other save the family business or put it in greater danger?

DANCE OF DESIRE is the first contemporary romance from award-winning, *New York Times* bestselling author Christopher Rice, told with the author's trademark humor and heart. It also introduces readers to a quirky and beautiful town in the Texas Hill Country called Chapel Springs.

READER ADVISORY. DANCE OF DESIRE contains fantasies

of dubious consent, acted on by consenting adults. Readers with sensitivities to those issues should be advised.

Desire & Ice
by Christopher Rice

Danny Patterson isn't a teenager anymore. He's the newest and youngest sheriff's deputy in Surrender, Montana. A chance encounter with his former schoolteacher on the eve of the biggest snowstorm to hit Surrender in years shows him that some schoolboy crushes never fade. Sometimes they mature into grown-up desire.

It's been years since Eliza Brightwell set foot in Surrender. So why is she back now? And why does she seem like she's running from something? To solve this mystery, Danny disobeys a direct order from Sheriff Cooper MacKenzie and sets out into a fierce blizzard, where his courage and his desire might be the only things capable of saving Eliza from a dark force out of her own past.

The Flame
By Christopher Rice

IT ONLY TAKES A MOMENT…

Cassidy Burke has the best of both worlds, a driven and successful husband and a wild, impulsive best friend. But after a decadent Mardi Gras party, Cassidy finds both men pulling away from her. Did the three of them awaken secret desires during a split-second of alcohol-fueled passion? Or is Mardi Gras a time when rules are meant to be broken without consequence?

Only one thing is for certain—the chill that's descended over her marriage, and her most important friendship, will soon turn into a deep freeze if she doesn't do something. And soon.

LIGHT THIS FLAME AT THE SCENE OF YOUR GREATEST PASSION AND ALL YOUR DESIRES WILL BE YOURS.

The invitation stares out at her from the window of a French Quarter boutique. The store's owner claims to have no knowledge of the strange candle. But Cassidy can't resist its intoxicating scent or the challenge written across its label in elegant cursive. With the strike of a match and one tiny flame, she will call forth a supernatural being with the ultimate power—the power to unchain the heart, the power to remove the fear that stands between a person and their truest desires.

The Surrender Gate
A Desire Exchange Novel
By Christopher Rice

Emily Blaine's life is about to change. Arthur Benoit, the kindly multimillionaire who has acted as her surrogate father for years, has just told her he's leaving her his entire estate, and he only has a few months to live. Soon Emily will go from being a restaurant manager with a useless English degree to the one of the richest and most powerful women in New Orleans. There's just one price. Arthur has written a letter to his estranged son Ryan he hopes will mend the rift between them, and he wants Emily to deliver the letter before it's too late. But finding Ryan won't be easy. He's been missing for years. He was recently linked to a mysterious organization called The Desire Exchange. But is The Desire Exchange just an urban legend? Or are the rumors true? Is it truly a secret club where the wealthy can live out their most private sexual fantasies?

It's a task Emily can't undertake alone. But there's only one man qualified to help her, her gorgeous and confident best friend, Jonathan Claiborne. She's suspected Jonathan of working as a high-priced escort for months now, and she's willing to bet that while giving pleasure to some of the most powerful men in New Orleans, Jonathan has uncovered some possible leads to The Desire Exchange—and to Ryan Benoit. But Emily's attempt to uncover Jonathan's secret life lands the two of them in hot water. Literally. In order to escape the clutches of one of Jonathan's most powerful and dangerous clients, they're forced to act on long buried desires—for each other.

When Emily's mission turns into an undercover operation, Jonathan insists on going with her. He also insists they continue to explore their impossible, reckless passion for each other. Enter Marcus Dylan, the hard-charging ex-Navy SEAL Arthur has hired to keep Emily safe. But Marcus has been hired for another reason. He, too, has a burning passion for Emily, a passion that might keep Emily from being distracted and confused by a best friend who claims he might be able to go straight just for her. But Marcus is as rough and controlling as Jonathan is sensual and reckless. As Emily searches for a place where the rich turn their fantasies into reality, she will be forced to decide which one of her own long-ignored fantasies should become her reality. But as Emily, Jonathan, and Marcus draw closer to The Desire Exchange itself, they find their destination isn't just shrouded in mystery, but in magic as well.

Kiss the Flame
A Desire Exchange Novella
By Christopher Rice

Are some risks worth taking?
Laney Foley is the first woman from her hard working family to attend college. That's why she can't act on her powerful attraction to one of the gorgeous teaching assistants in her Introduction to Art History course. Getting involved with a man who has control over her final grade is just too risky. But ever since he first laid eyes on her, Michael Brouchard seems to think about little else but the two of them together. And it's become harder for Laney to ignore his intelligence and his charm.

During a walk through the French Quarter, an intoxicating scent that reminds Laney of her not-so-secret admirer draws her into an elegant scented candle shop. The shop's charming and mysterious owner seems to have stepped out of another time, and he offers Laney a gift that could break down the walls of her fear in a way that can only be described as magic. But will she accept it?

Light this flame at the scene of your greatest passion and all your desires will be yours...

Lilliane Williams is a radiant, a supernatural being with the power to make your deepest sexual fantasy take shape around you with just a gentle press of her lips to yours. But her gifts came at a price. Decades ago, she set foot inside what she thought was an ordinary scented candle shop in the French Quarter. When she resisted the magical gift offered to her inside, Lilliane was endowed with eternal youth and startling supernatural powers, but the ability to experience and receive romantic love was removed from her forever. When Lilliane meets a young woman who seems poised to make the same mistake she did years before, she becomes determined to stop her, but that will mean revealing her truth to a stranger. Will Lilliane's story provide Laney with the courage she needs to open her heart to the kind of true love only magic can reveal?

About Christopher Rice
writing as C. Travis Rice

C. Travis Rice is the pen name *New York Times* Bestselling Author Christopher Rice devotes to steamy tales of passion, intrigue, and romance between men. An executive producer for television, he has published multiple bestselling books in multiple genres and received a Lambda Literary Award. Together with his best friend and producing partner, *New York Times* Bestselling Author Eric Shaw Quinn, he runs the production company Dinner Partners. Among other projects, they produce the podcast and video network, TDPS, which you can find at www.TheDinnerPartyShow.com. Head over to VisitSapphireCove.com to learn about the Sapphire Cove series. Learn more about C. Travis Rice and Christopher Rice at www.christopherricebooks.com.

On Behalf of Blue Box Press,

Liz Berry and Jillian Stein would like to thank ~

Steve Berry
Benjamin Stein
Kim Guidroz
Chelle Olson
Tanaka Kangara
Ann-Marie Nieves
Grace Wenk
Asha Hossain
Chris Graham
Jessica Saunders
Stacey Tardif
Suzy Baldwin
Dylan Stockton
Kate Boggs
Richard Blake
and Simon Lipskar